Five years ago Simon Durant had been Victoria's knight-errant. She had trusted him with her love, only to have him shatter her world. Now he was a memory—and a story that Victoria was determined to write, with or without his co-operation...

*Books you will enjoy
by AVERY THORNE*

NO OTHER CHANCE

A talented and dedicated actress, Livia Paige was thrilled when she landed a part in a new play with the celebrated actor Jonathan Worth. But she was not so thrilled when Jonathan began to show every sign of being romantically interested with her. Wasn't she being rather foolish to be so determined to put her career before her love life?

A SPLENDID PASSION

When the famous actor and film star Julian Tremain invited up-and-coming actress Kate Reid to London to do a play with him, she was delighted—from a career point of view, but wary of getting emotionally involved with a womaniser like Julian. But she needn't have worried ...

SAFELY TO TRUST

BY
AVERY THORNE

MILLS & BOON LIMITED
15–16 BROOK'S MEWS
LONDON W1A 1DR

All the characters in this book have no existence outside the imagination of the Author, and have no relation whatsoever to anyone bearing the same name or names. They are not even distantly inspired by any individual known or unknown to the Author, and all the incidents are pure invention.

The text of this publication or any part thereof may not be reproduced or transmitted in any form or by any means, electronic or mechanical, including photocopying, recording, storage in an information retrieval system, or otherwise, without the written permission of the publisher.

This book is sold subject to the condition that it shall not, by way of trade or otherwise, be lent, resold, hired out or otherwise circulated without the prior consent of the publisher in any form of binding or cover other than that in which it is published and without a similar condition including this condition being imposed on the subsequent purchaser.

*First published in Great Britain 1985
by Mills & Boon Limited*

© Avery Thorne 1985

*Australian copyright 1985
Philippine copyright 1985
This edition 1985*

ISBN 0 263 75093 0

*Set in Monophoto Times 10 on 11 pt.
01-0785 – 55045*

*Made and printed in Great Britain by
Richard Clay (The Chaucer Press) Ltd,
Bungay, Suffolk*

CHAPTER ONE

VICTORIA was following the conversation with only half an ear. It had been a long day for her, and the evening showed every indication of being even longer. Ken Newsome's arrival in town that day had provided all the excuse necessary for the party which was now in full swing. The international staff members of the Global News Service office in New York were always happy to have an excuse for a party, an opportunity to talk shop without the pressure of deadlines.

Victoria always joined the parties, because these people were her co-workers and her friends, although the friendships were mostly detached and casual. Still, she enjoyed the company and the easy comradeship which bound the staff together. She usually had a good time at the parties, but tonight was an exception.

She didn't really like Ken, and never had. It irritated her that he was dominating the conversation to such an extent, describing his experiences in great detail. The others were clearly fascinated, and Victoria supposed that Ken did have interesting things to say. He had just returned from a month of the sort of high adventure any reporter would find irresistible. He'd been in Afghanistan, with the rebel forces who were fighting the Russian troops occupying the country. He was full of talk of commando raids, frontal assaults, helicopter gunships and mountain strongholds.

Victoria might have been interested, too, had Ken's attitude not been a little too condescending. It almost seemed that he'd invented the war between the rebels and the Russian troops. If the rebels had been winning—which they clearly weren't—Ken probably would have taken credit for the victory. Instead, he modestly accepted praise for his bravery under fire and his bulldog tenacity in pursuit of a story which, he said solemnly, *had* to be told.

Victoria found that comment particularly amusing. Ken surely knew as well as she that the story already *had* been told, and that any number of other reporters had been into Afghanistan to gather firsthand accounts of the fighting. Ken's exploits were hardly unique, but that fact didn't seem to deter him in the least.

Nothing ever deterred Ken, Victoria told herself with cynical amusement. He was too sure of himself, too smug. She'd long since decided that his inflated sense of self-importance was nothing more than overcompensation. He was a small man, thin and wiry and not much more than her own height. Ken's problem was that he didn't fit his image of himself. He needed to be at least a foot taller, so he could tower over everyone else in a room. He needed to be a romantic and adventuresome figure and—since he couldn't *look* like one—he was determined to *be* one.

But being a romantic and adventuresome figure took more than force of will, Victoria thought to herself. She'd known one, once, and he had commanded attention and respect without any effort. There had been a lived-in, almost worn, air about him, as though he'd seen and done a great deal more than most people, and had been touched by it all. That was what made a person into a romantic and adventuresome figure: the ability to be touched by what one saw and did.

'You don't seem overly impressed by our foreign correspondent.'

It took Victoria a moment to pull herself away from the past, to leave the memory behind. But some memories were dangerous, and she was grateful for the interruption as she turned her attention to her boss, Tim Sanders. He was a huge bear of a man, with a wonderful gentleness about him and a puckish sense of humour which was often on display.

'Aren't you impressed?' he asked. 'You're supposed to be.'

'I'm impressed that he got out alive,' Victoria answered blithely. 'It's a wonder the rebels didn't drive a stake through his heart.'

'The mujahideen,' Tim corrected. 'You're not supposed to call them rebels. They're the mujahideen—the holy worriors.'

'I know,' she agreed wearily. 'Speaking Pathan or Pushtu—or whatever it is they speak—and slipping through the Khyber Pass under cover of darkness, and fighting Ken's holy war for him.'

'Or was he fighting theirs for them?'

'I suppose it all depends on whether you ask Ken or the mujahideen.' She paused to watch him for a moment. 'I'm not being very kind, am I?' she asked, turning back to Tim.

'I don't care if you're kind or not, but you should be listening with rapt attention. Play your cards right, Vicky, and the great man may take you home tonight.'

'Then *I'd* have to drive the stake through his heart.'

'Or let him have his way with you,' Tim suggested. 'I get the distinct impression that he'd like to have his way with you.'

'If that's true, it's just because I've never been impressed by him. He can't stand to think there's a woman who isn't.'

'That's part of it, I suppose.' Tim took a moment to objectively study Victoria. She wasn't a bad-looking woman, although she was a little too thin for his taste. He supposed he ought to call her slender, but thin seemed more accurate. She was a little above average height, small boned, with nice but understated curves. He knew for a fact that she was twenty-seven, but she looked considerably younger—like a girl just out of school. She had dark hair, cut short and curling casually around her face, emphasising fine features and the clearest grey eyes he'd ever seen. But she always looked too thin, he thought regretfully, as though she ran more on nervous energy than food. If she had been more his type, he would have taken her out to dinner every night, to put a little meat on her bones. As it was, he enjoyed their friendship and shared sense of the ridiculous. 'You might give him credit for having good taste,' Tim finally observed, breaking his silence.

'I'd rather not,' Victoria said firmly. 'I'd rather not give him any credit at all, but I know he is a good reporter.'

'Of course he is,' Tim agreed sourly. 'I don't like him, either, but he's good.'

Victoria knew Ken was an excellent reporter, although she hated to acknowledge that fact. She turned back to listen to him again, hearing him expounding now on the Panjshir Valley. 'That seems to be the key, at the moment,' he was explaining. 'That's where the mujahideen are having their greatest success. They've got a lot of men involved up there, better organisation, and strong leadership. They're driving the Russians crazy. There may even be some U.S. involvement in the area—at least on a limited basis.'

'But we're not providing any support,' someone said flatly.

'Not officially,' Ken agreed with a knowing smile, 'but I've got to check with some of my sources in Washington. I know for a fact that there was one American operating in the area—advising some of the guerrilla units and fighting with them. They were using classic guerrilla methods with considerable success, and he was very much in charge. There were rumours about him all over the valley. They called him the blue-eyed American chief.'

'Are you sure he wasn't a reporter, too?' someone asked.

'That man was no reporter,' Ken said with conviction. 'He was definitely a fighter. He came into our camp one night, with a group of his men. I got a good look at him before he realised that I was an American reporter. Then he was furious and made himself scarce in one hell of a hurry. He sure didn't want to talk to a reporter.'

'Ken refuses to take these things personally,' Tim observed, waiting for Victoria to appreciate the joke.

But she wasn't listening to Tim. She was staring intently at Ken, her expression suddenly watchful.

'A mercenary?' someone asked. 'One of those crazy soldiers of fortune in search of a good war to fight?'

'Could be,' Ken agreed, 'but I haven't heard of any others. There doesn't seem to be enough money involved to attract that bunch. That's what makes me wonder if the C.I.A. isn't providing a little unofficial assistance.'

'I don't suppose you heard his name?' Victoria asked, moving a step closer.

'The night he came into camp, I heard someone calling him Sahmid or Samin—something like that.' Ken eyed her with curiosity. 'It sounded like a Moslem name, but the man was no Moslem. Why?' he asked with a smile that bordered on sarcasm. 'Do you think you know him?'

'I might know who he is,' she answered, trying to appear nonchalant as she fought a sudden rush of emotion. 'I *have* acquired a few contacts of my own. What did he look like?' she persisted.

'Tall, dark hair, clean shaven. The thing I noticed

most were light blue eyes. Come on, Vicky—who do you think he is? Or what?'

She shrugged. 'I'm not sure. He might be someone I interviewed, a long time ago.' She had hesitated briefly before she used the word 'interviewed', but she didn't think anyone had noticed.

'But what is he?' Ken demanded. 'An agent, or a mercenary?'

'That's *my* story, isn't it?' she asked with a malicious smile. 'You don't think I'm going to give it away, do you?'

'I don't see what you're going to do with it,' Ken pointed out, irritated. 'He's a hell of a long way away, and you haven't got any contacts there. You can't do anything with it, and I might be able to.'

'But you've got so much to work with,' Victoria told him. 'All I've got is one interesting little angle. You don't begrudge me that, do you?'

'I do, if you've got something to link him to the C.I.A.,' Ken said. 'That would be important, Vicky. You can't just play around with something like that!'

'If he's the man I think he might be, he's got nothing to do with the C.I.A.—nothing at all to do with the government. He'd be strictly independent.'

'And I suppose he'd have told you that, wouldn't he?' Ken asked sarcastically. ' "What me? Something to do with the government? Certainly not!" And you'd have believed it, of course! That's what I can't stand about women who think they're newsmen,' he continued, turning away from Victoria to address the rest of the group. 'They don't deal with facts—they go on instinct and emotion.'

Victoria would have liked to debate that point. She was sick to death of male chauvinists—and Ken was one of the worst—who continually put down women in the news profession. But it seemed more diplomatic, at the moment, to avoid the issue. 'I'll tell you what,' she said, forcing herself to give Ken one of her nicest smiles. 'I'll do a little checking and then let you know, if there's anything I think you could use—or anything I don't understand,' she added as a deliberate sop to his vanity.

'I hope you do.' He eyed her with active dislike.

'But there may be nothing to it at all,' she continued brightly. 'Just a silly, emotional whim of mine. I shouldn't have interrupted you—not when you've got so much to tell. You go ahead, and I'll just listen.'

That had mollified him at least slightly, she saw with relief. She moved back a step as he took up the thread of his story, forging steadily on through the Panjshir Valley as he explained the latest Russian offensive.

'Vicky, you are the most incredible hypocrite,' Tim said softly, leaning forward to make himself heard.

'I know,' she agreed apologetically, 'but sometimes I need to be.'

'And will you tell me what this all about?'

She nodded. 'Sometime. But I think I'd better listen attentively for a while. That might help.'

'Short of kissing his feet, nothing's going to help,' Tim kidded. 'I think you'd better let me take you home, or Ken will drive a stake through *your* heart.'

'Yes, but let me listen for a little longer,' she insisted. The Panjshir Valley had suddenly captured her attention, even if she had to hear about it from Ken.

She filed away scraps of information: the Hindu Kush Mountains, the Russian airbase at Bagram, the saturation bombing of the villages, the mountain caves where the guerrilla fighters found relative safety. She began to be able to picture the night-time commando raids, the brief engagements followed by quick retreats back into the mountains, the impossibility of trying to bring down Russian helicopter gunships with small arms fire.

It suddenly mattered, and Victoria wasn't prepared—not just yet—to question the advisability of allowing it to matter. For years, she hadn't known where Simon was. Now she had an eerie sense of knowing exactly where he was—but only if she were right in her suspicions. It might be nothing but coincidence; it was almost bound to be. The world was so random that Ken couldn't possibly have wandered into a camp in Afghanistan and met a man Victoria had known for several years.

But it was hard to explain away the small clues in what Ken had said. Afghanistan was just the sort of place that would attract Simon. Fighting with the rebels—the mujahideen, she corrected quickly—was exactly what she'd expect of him. But there was more to it than that. Ken had said they called the American the blue-eyed chief and had commented specifically on the man's light blue eyes. Anyone who had ever seen Simon was going to remember and remark on his eyes. Ken said the man was tall, with dark hair, and it was true that a lot of men could be described that way. But how many of them could be found in Afghanistan, doing precisely what she would expect Simon to be doing? And Ken had heard them call him Sahmid or Samin.

She experimented silently with the sounds. Sahmid, Samin, Simon. Coincidence suddenly seemed stretched painfully thin. Had a group of Afghan guerrillas corrupted Simon's name to give it a more familiar sound? It seemed likely; it fitted well with the rest that Ken had told her.

'You're not listening,' Tim pointed out. 'You're miles away. Come on—I'll take you home.'

'You don't need to. I've got cab fare.'

'I don't care if you've got cab fare. I want to hear what this is all about. Come on,' he repeated, taking her firmly by the arm and leading her towards the door.

'What *is* this all about?' he persisted, once they were settled in a cab. 'You were beginning to look as though someone had walked over your grave, just before we left.'

'Not quite so bad as that,' Victoria said self-consciously, wondering how much she ought to say, or wanted to say—or even think—about the present reality of Simon. 'It's just that a bell rang, when Ken began to talk about that American.'

'Some one you interviewed,' Tim said sceptically.

'Years ago,' she agreed, staring out the cab window.

'You haven't been in this business that long, Vicky. And even if you had been, I don't believe for a minute that you're thinking about someone who was nothing more than an interview.'

'Why do you say that?' she asked impatiently, brushing the curls from her forehead with a quick, nervous gesture.

'Because it's not like you to force the issue, and you did force it to a fair extent, with Ken.'

'Asking a few simple questions isn't forcing the issue!'

'It is, when it's done the way you did it. It's not your style to flat out ask questions. Your style is to drift into a conversation and make a couple of casual observations. Suddenly the person you're talking to is either agreeing or disagreeing with tremendous conviction, and adding an incredible amount of detail. That's what makes you such a good interviewer—people don't realise what you're doing to them.'

'Well, I could hardly drift into Ken's conversation, could I?' she asked reasonably. 'If you want to learn something from Ken, you're got to ask him fast, before he's on to something else.'

'I suppose you're right about that,' Tim agreed thoughtfully. 'But that begs the question of why you wanted to learn anything from Ken. You hadn't even been following what he had to say, and then you suddenly came alive—wanting to know all about this strange American.'

'I thought I might know who he was.'

'And then,' Tim went on, ignoring her comment, 'you did your little self-effacing act and took in every blessed word he had to say about the Panjshir Valley, which is where your American happens to be.'

'He's not *my* American!'

'And once Ken had left the Panjshir Valley behind,' Tim continued with dogged determination, 'you stopped listening completely. You were trying to work something out, and that's when you began to look as though someone had just walked over your grave. Who's the ghost, Vicky?'

'It's not a ghost! It's just that it sounded like it could be someone I met a few years ago. It seemed like a strange coincidence—that's all.'

'A hell of a one,' Tim agreed cheerfully. 'How did you ever come to meet the kind of man who commands guerrilla units in Afghanistan?'

'But I don't even know if it *is* the same man, and he wasn't commanding guerrilla units in Afghanistan when I met him.'

'I'd already figured that one out. But——' he hesitated as the cab drew over to the side of the street. 'Invite me up for coffee, and you can tell me all about it,' he suggested with an engaging grin. 'If you don't, you'll lie awake all night, thinking about it.' He handed the driver the fare and then waited while Victoria unlocked the outside door. 'I'm glad to see the lock still works,' he noted, eying the run-down building with mild distaste.

Once a factory, the building now housed a grocery store on the ground floor. Above, the other four stories had been converted into a rabbit's warren of small apartments. The hallways were shabby with peeling paint and years of accumulated grim, and the freight elevator was rarely in operation. Still, Victoria enjoyed living there. The tenants were a relatively stable group, a nice mix of young professional people like herself and a few retired people who took a friendly interest in their neighbours.

'It's not as bad as you think,' Victoria told him firmly, starting up the stairs. On the second landing, they dodged a child's stroller and continued on. 'It's a very nice place.'

'And a hell of a climb,' he observed, already a little out of breath. 'No wonder you're so thin—having to do these stairs all the time. Doesn't that elevator ever work?'

'Not very often,' she admitted as they reached the top floor and stopped at her door. 'Besides, it's so slow that it's hardly worth the effort.' She unlocked the door and switched on the light. 'What do you want? Coffee or cheap wine?'

'Coffee. Your cheap wine's too cheap for me.' He stopped to catch his breath, looking around the place and thinking—as he always did—how much it looked like Victoria.

It was one large room, except for a kitchen alcove and the partitioned off corner which housed a tiny bath and an even smaller closet. Like Victoria, the living space was quiet and understated, with pale walls and a complete absence of clutter. Against one wall a day bed doubled as a couch, facing two arm chairs across the square coffee table which was bare except for a neatly stacked pile of magazines. The opposite wall was lined with bookshelves, the books neatly arranged by subject and author. There wasn't any other furniture in the room, except for an antique bureau—yellow with brown stencilling, with a matching mirror above it—

and Victoria's table. Victoria's table was something to behold. A good ten feet long, it was of sturdy oak and highly polished. On it she had her typewriter, her telephone, her neat pile of file folders, a coffee mug which held a collection of pens and pencils, and always—winter and summer—a cut glass vase with flowers in it. The table was placed against the line of floor to ceiling windows which made up the fourth wall of the room.

There were no curtains at the windows, just a collection of hanging plants and ratten blinds which could be lowered when the sun slanted in on hot summer days. Over the couch hung a fabric wall hanging in shades of beige and brown and gold, complimenting the beige cover on the couch and the two gold arm chairs. Another wall was devoted to Victoria's collection of gravestone rubbings. To Tim, they were anything but cheerful—all grinning death's heads or weeping willows and funeral urns, with a couple of slightly more optimistic cherubs thrown in for good measure. He supposed that they had artistic merit and he knew that Victoria enjoyed making them, but they weren't what he'd have chosen for his walls.

' "Here lies interred ye remains of Mrs Susanna Rawson",' he read aloud from one of the rubbings, " 'wife of ye Reverend William Rawson. Died May ye sixteenth, 1748 in ye seventy-second year of her age." ' Tim broke off to look at Victoria. 'That's got to be the strangest damn thing anyone's ever hung on a wall!'

'Simon liked it,' Victoria said without thinking. She'd been spooning instant coffee into mugs, remembering the night five years before when she'd offered Simon a choice of cheap wine or coffee. Now she was suddenly reminded of the next afternoon in the graveyard, when he had seen the original of Susanna's stone. 'He liked it very much,' she finished softly.

'So that's his name!' Tim looked more intently at her. 'Simon. Simon, Sahmid, Samin.' As Victoria had earlier, he tried the three names experimentally. 'So it is the same man.'

'Well, I can't be sure of that, can I?' she asked, waiting for the water to boil.

'It's one hell of a coincidence, if it isn't the same man. I assume your Simon was tall and dark, with blue eyes?'

'He wasn't *my* Simon,' Victoria said bitterly.

'Perhaps you thought he was,' Tim suggested kindly. 'Did something go wrong?'

'I was mistaken about him,' she answered obliquely.

'Ah.' Tim paused to think that over for a minute. 'Were you very young?'

'I don't think so. I was twenty-two.' The kettle began to whistle and she turned off the gas and then poured water into the mugs.

'You probably were a very young twenty-two,' Tim observed wisely. 'You were still pretty young when you came to work for me a year later.'

'I don't see what that has to do with it,' she said impatiently. She handed him one of the mugs and settled on the couch while he took the chair across from her.

'Well, he must have been a pretty strange character. It stands to reason—anyone who ends up five years later, fighting with Afghan rebels can't be average. Besides, if he liked those crazy gravestones of yours, he *had* to be strange. Perhaps you were too young for someone that different. But that's not the point, is it?' he continued hastily, seeing the sudden defiant set to her features. 'It doesn't really matter what went wrong, or why. What I don't understand is how you ever managed to meet someone like this man.'

'He was a friend of a friend,' Victoria explained briefly.

'Was he already involved in things as exotic as going off to Afghanistan to fight with rebels?'

'Yes. If it *is* the same person.'

'Lord, it's got to be the same person. Same name—more or less—looks the same. He sounds like a bloody movie star—tall, dark and handsome. Somehow I wouldn't have expected you to go for the movie star type. I think of you as distrusting romantic figures.'

'He wasn't at all like a movie star,' she said without thinking. 'He was interesting to look at, and very interesting to talk to, but nothing like a movie star. I suppose he was a sort of romantic figure,' she added reluctantly, knowing there was no 'suppose' about it.

'But——' Tim prompted.

'But what?'

'There's more to this story than the ghost of Christmas Past,' he explained. 'Are you considering the possibility of rekindling a romance with someone half a world away?'

'Of course not,' she said crossly.

'Then why are you so interested?'

'Because there might be a story in it—if the man really is Simon.'

'A story you won't give to Ken.'

'Of course I won't give it to Ken,' she answered indignantly. 'He's never done me any favours; I'm not about to start doing any for him. Besides, it's *my* story, if I can prove it.'

'Is he government connected?' Tim asked softly, leaning forward. He trusted Victoria as a thorough investigative reporter, skilled at picking up on the most subtle points and pursuing them relentlessly. If she suspected a connection, or if she knew one existed, she'd find confirmation. 'There would be a real story in that. The government denies any direct involvement in Afghanistan. All we've done for the Afghans thus far is boycott the 1980 Olympics—a fact which must have boosted their morale no end. I know the government wouldn't mind seeing Russia thoroughly tied up and embarrassed by the fighting there, but nothing is being done to promote it through the use of advisers. There's enough of a problem with American advisers in Central America. It could prove awkward, if even one were discovered to be operating with the rebels in Afghanistan.'

'It's not government connected,' Victoria said, surprised at how quickly her mind was moving. When the thought had first come to her that Ken might be talking about Simon, she'd only been able to concentrate on the personal aspects—what Simon had once meant to her. But now she realised how much more there might be. A germ of an idea had been growing, even while she talked to Tim. She was remembering fragments of conversation, random comments, things she'd read and things she'd heard. A lot of them were beginning to fit together. 'It would be more of a feature story. I'm not sure if you'd call it human interest or hard news. A little of both, I think.'

'I don't have the slightest idea what you're talking about,' Tim said with a puzzled expression. 'Are you sure you don't still have a crush on this man?'

'Women don't have crushes anymore,' she corrected firmly. 'Don't date yourself. Even if they did, I can assure you that I haven't one. This is something very different.' She stopped, thinking rapidly through her half-formed ideas. 'I'd need to do a lot of digging,' she finally resumed. 'I'd have to do a lot here at this end, and I'd need to know everything I could about the man Ken saw. Is there any way I could get that?'

'Ken might be able to tell you more,' Tim suggested.

'Some, perhaps, but that's not what I need. I'd need to know more about the kinds of things he's doing—

what other people think of him. Something more concrete. Is there any way we can get information out of Afghanistan?' she asked, thinking of the vast resources of Global News.

'It would help if you'd thought of this before Ken went in there,' Tim pointed out. 'He was on the spot and could have found a lot for you. But we're not going to send him back just because you've got some vague idea—which, by the way, means nothing to me.'

'Well, there's no reason why it should. I'm not even sure it means anything to me. But, if you'd give me a couple of days—just let me dig around for a day or two——' she fixed him with her clear grey eyes,' —I'll know if I'm on to something or not. Will you give me a couple of days?'

'And what happens after your couple of days?'

'I'll give you what I know, and you can decide if it's worth any additional effort.'

'But you think it might be,' Tim mused.

'I know it *will* be—if I'm right. News and human interest.' She sat back, threading her fingers through her short curls. 'It's a story a lot of people have been looking for,' she continued, a far-away look in her eyes. 'Over the years, there has been a lot of speculation, but no one has ever proved a thing. I don't believe anyone has ever suspected a thing. And the joke of it is that I may have been sitting on the story, for the last five years.' She shook her head ruefully.

'I don't know what the hell you're talking about!'

'You will, in a couple of days. Then I'll tell you what I have, and you can decide if you want me to follow it.'

'You *are* kind,' he murmured, favouring her with a sardonic smile. 'I'm your boss—remember? I always make the decisions. But what am I going to have to do—*if* I decide to let you follow this story?'

'Get me information from Afghanistan. Can you?'

'A certain amount. I suppose,' he agreed, thinking quickly. 'We've got a stringer in Peshawar. I expect he could turn up something.'

'Where is that?' Victoria asked quickly.

'You weren't listening to Ken, and, for someone who thinks she's got a hot story about an American in Afghanistan, you show an abysmal lack of knowledge of the territory. Peshawar is in Pakistan, just across the border from Afghanistan. It's at one end of the Khyber Pass, and serves as a sort of staging area for the rebels. There are refugee camps nearby, and some of them are almost rear-echelon bases for the rebels. There's also a Red Cross hospital there, and some of the wounded guerrilla fighters make it back there for care. Most of the news that gets out of Afghanistan comes through Peshawar. If anyone knows about your strange American, our stringer ought to be able to find out.'

'Well, that's something.' Victoria nodded approvingly. 'And don't worry about my abysmal lack of knowledge. By the end of the week, I'll be an expert on Peshawar and everything else to do with the area.' She smiled as she said it, but her face suddenly displayed an interesting combination of self-confidence and grim determination.

'I know you will,' Tim agreed cheerfully, having already had several opportunities to observe Victoria's ability to grasp a great deal of information in a short period of time. 'All right.' He nodded, setting down his empty mug and getting to his feet. 'I'll give you a couple of days.'

'Thanks,' she said briefly as she followed him to the door.

'Tell me one thing,' he directed, pausing with his hand on the knob. 'You've been talking about someone who obviously meant a great deal to you, at least at one time. Now he's suddenly become a story—with a capital S. How come?'

'Just for that reason,' she answered calmly. 'Because I think he may be a story—with a capital S.'

'Nothing more than that?' he asked sceptically. 'No faint notion of renewing old acquaintance? No hope that the story might bring the two of you together again?'

'None at all. If I'm right, the last thing in the world he'd want is to have his story told.'

'Then why do it?' Tim asked reasonably. 'Is it just for the story, or would there be a little element of revenge mixed in?'

'There's a lot of revenge mixed in, as a matter of fact,' she told him without a trace of emotion. 'Five years ago, we were planning to get married.'

'And things went wrong,' Tim supplied helpfully. 'There finally came the inevitable scene, with all the inevitable recriminations, and that was the end of it.'

'It wasn't as simple as that,' Victoria said without emotion. 'We had the big scene, because he was leaving and I didn't want him to go. But he assured me that he'd be back in three months, and we'd be married then.'

'And he never came back?' Tim asked, watching her face.

'No. He came back about a year later,' she answered evenly, 'thinking we could pick up where we left off. The point was that he had no intention of marrying me. His other life mattered more to him than I did. He just wanted to use me, when it suited his convenience.' She smiled briefly, an impersonal smile. 'Now it's my turn. If I can, I'm going to use him for all it's worth.'

Tim nodded, because there was nothing he could say. But he wished Victoria hadn't explained things with such cool self-possession. Then it came to him that

Victoria was always cool and self-possessed; it was only that he'd never known why. Now that he did know, he was left feeling depressed and wishing he could say something to help. But Victoria didn't want any help; it was obvious that he couldn't do anything for her. So he said good night and left.

After she'd closed the door, Victoria methodically picked up the two mugs and carried them to the sink. There was no change in her expression as she washed them and set them in the drainer. But inside, she felt torn apart by too many conflicting emotions—more than she could possibly handle.

Simon was suddenly real again, and that frightened her. For years, she'd kept the reality at bay, had allowed herself to think of him only infrequently and then only with careful detachment. But now it was obvious that he'd always been there. It seemed incredible that, after all these years, she might have found him again. Even more incredible was the fact that she had been looking for him during those years. In her reading and her thinking, in her insatiable interest in people, she had always been looking for Simon. Without being aware of it, she had been storing up countless impressions, and this evening had been the catalyst, the final piece she needed to fit all the other pieces into place. It was frightening to realise the extent to which he had consumed her.

When she was ready for bed, she paused for a moment to study her reflection in the mirror above the stencilled bureau. She didn't look any different, she realised with surprise. None of what she was feeling showed in her face. She looked calm and controlled and in complete possession of herself. She was torn apart by love and hate, but none of it showed.

For years, she hadn't allowed herself to remember how much she had once loved Simon. Nor had she allowed herself to recognise how much anger and bitterness he'd left behind. How could a man create such a conflict of feelings? she silently asked her reflection. But there wasn't any real answer to that question, except to acknowledge the reality of Simon.

He was, and always had been, a great deal more than just a man. He'd been a force she couldn't resist, a mass of contradictions and fascinating contrasts. He'd captured her imagination; he'd captured her soul. The spell wasn't broken yet. It was all still there. As she turned away from the mirror and switched off the light, the memories came flooding back. They were fresh and new again and she lay awake for hours, trapped by them, unable to escape.

CHAPTER TWO

VICTORIA had been watching him even before he came to her rescue, aware of him because he was so different from the others at Joel and Mira's party. In a room where everyone was upwardly mobile, this stranger was quite the reverse. His clothing wasn't smart or trendy; there were no designer labels or little alligators in evidence. He was wearing faded jeans and a knit shirt which had obviously seen better days. The jeans did have the advantage of emphasising his long, lean form, and the blue of his shirt almost precisely matched his eyes. They were unusual eyes, very light but unmistakeably blue, their colour even more pronounced against his dark hair and deeply tanned skin.

Mira had said he was a friend of Joel's—the reason, or at least the excuse, for this particular party—but he didn't look like a friend of Joel's. There was nothing cleverly academic about him, and it didn't appear that casual chatter and quick laughter were his strong suits. Victoria had the feeling that he wasn't enjoying himself any more than she was, but it was obvious that he wasn't in the least intimidated by anyone.

For that she envied him. She felt totally out of her depth at this party; she hadn't yet acquired the brittle veneer which passed as self-confidence and which she would learn to use to carry her through occasions of this sort. She was still painfully shy and unsure of herself, easily intimidated by the clever people who were Joel's friends. Like Joel, they were mostly members of the Political Science Department at Dartmouth, and all frighteningly academic types.

She hadn't even wanted to come to the party; Mira had forced her into it. First, Mira wanted her at the party because she needed someone literate. Joel had said his friend was terribly literate, that Mira should try to get some literate people together for the party. As Mira had pointed out, Victoria more than qualified, because she'd had two short stories published.

Besides, Mira had continued brightly when issuing the invitation, Victoria had to come so that Linda could go home with her. Linda was Mira's old roommate, and Mira had invited her for the week-end. But that was before Joel's friend had got in touch with them and Joel had decided that the friend must spend the weekend there. That meant there wouldn't be any room for Linda in the tiny apartment, so she had to go somewhere else. 'And, since, you and Linda are friends, and you've got plenty of room....' Mira had left the words hanging, waiting for Victoria to agree to take Linda in for the weekend.

'My car's in the shop for repairs,' Victoria had explained truthfully, relieved to have an excuse to avoid the party. She'd had one taste of the kind of party Mira and Joel gave, and didn't relish another. Nor did she want to spend a weekend with Linda, with whom she had nothing in common. 'I won't be able to come.'

'Of course you will,' Mira had said firmly, refusing to allow her plans to be destroyed. 'Linda's got her car, and she can pick you up and the two of you can go back to your place together. It's a perfect arrangement!'

So Victoria had been trapped into coming, but she had quickly retreated to the edge of the room so she wouldn't have to try to make conversation. She was content to watch the general activity, although it was Joel's friend who particularly fascinated her. He obviously possessed the self-confidence she lacked and she was wondering how he'd managed to acquire it when she realised that Mira had suddenly decided to take her in hand.

Victoria found herself being drawn into the nearest knot of people, Mira explaining about the two stories. 'But they aren't exactly popular,' Mira finished casually. 'They're terribly obscure and she'll never be a success unless she changes her style.'

'But she will be.' It was Joel's friend, suddenly materialising beside Victoria. He had a lazy drawl, the hint of some vague regional accent she couldn't identify. 'She's very good, you know. I think she'll be quite successful before she's done.'

'I didn't realise,' Mira said, sounding properly impressed. 'You should have told me, Vicky!'

'But she wouldn't,' the stranger said quickly. He smiled down at Victoria, his eyes lit with amusement, as though the two of them were sharing a private joke. 'She's much too modest, which is part of her charm as a writer. Very unassuming, very low-key, with a marvellous subtlety to her work. You really ought to read her.'

Victoria had listened in fascination as he had come to her defence with such conviction. Later she would tell herself that it had been at that first moment that Simon had begun the process of enchanting her, of leaving her completely open to the hurt he would later inflict. But she hadn't known that at the time. She'd simply been dazzled and comforted by his unexpected defence of her, and quite literally breathless as he had slipped his hand under her arm and detached the two of them from the group.

'Thank you for being so kind,' she said shyly as they reached a quiet corner of the room. 'You're very flattering—good for my ego.'

'But it's no more than the truth, is it?' he asked,

leaning comfortably against the wall and fixing her with his light blue eyes.

'I don't know,' she answered distractedly, finding it difficult to concentrate while subjected to his careful scrutiny. '*I* don't think I'll ever be a success.'

'Doesn't it all depend on how one measures success? I don't expect these people——' he gestured briefly to the room '—measure it the way we would.' He broke off to study the others, regarding a private spectacle through narrowed eyes.

Because he was unaware of her for the moment, Victoria had a fine opportunity to study him. He was fascinating to look at—not conventionally handsome, but something she found infinitely more attractive. His face suggested a pen-and-ink sketch brought to life: finely drawn with a minimum of detail which served to reveal the strong bone structure beneath the flesh. In repose, it was an aristocratic face, with something like a touch of arrogance to it. When he smiled, it was completely different—approachable and engaging.

He looked like an active, outdoor person. She didn't think his tan came from lazy days on the beach, and the fine lines around his eyes suggested that he'd been exposed to extremes of heat and cold. She had a fanciful image of him doing exciting things; demanding things. There wasn't a spare ounce of flesh on his long frame, and he conveyed a sense of strength and quick reflexes.

He reminded her of a knight-errant, she suddenly realised, a wanderer in search of adventure. But not just adventure, she corrected. Like the knights-errant of medieval times, he was also chivalrous; he'd come to her rescue, hadn't he? And, like a knight-errant, he certainly looked capable of proving himself in battle.

'What's your name?' he asked suddenly, turning back to her and catching her in the act of studying his face.

'My name,' Victoria repeated blankly, trying to shift from the idea of a knight-errant to something as prosaic as her name. 'But you know my name,' she protested after an instant's thought. 'You've read my stuff.'

'I expect I have,' he said calmly, 'because it's safe to say that I read just about everything. But I won't know what it is of yours I've read until I know your name.'

'Do you mean to say that you went on about me to the others, when you don't even know my name?' She was captivated by the idea.

'I'm afraid so.' He smiled apologetically. 'It's a habit of mine—to get involved in something I know nothing about and pull it off successfully.'

'So you just made it all up,' she supplied dryly.

'I suppose you could say so,' he agreed cheerfully. 'I make assumptions, and I'm usually right. I'll know if I am about you, if you tell me your name,' He looked expectantly down at her.

'I'm Victoria Ward.'

'Are you really?' he asked slowly, his drawl suddenly more pronounced. He frowned briefly and then grinned. 'You can't be,' he said decisively. 'It's impossible. Victoria Ward is seventy, if she's a day. And a spinster.' He studied her more closely. 'You are a mere child,' he added accusingly.

'I'm twenty-two,' she protested.

'That *is* a mere child, as far as I'm concerned.' He smiled ruefully. 'Good lord! I've just been caught with a totally wrong assumption. I've been picturing you as a spare old Yankee—nothing grandmotherly or plump about you—with white hair in an untidy bun. A nice smile, though, and a knowing look of amusement.' He studied Victoria for another moment. 'You'll probably look a great deal like her in another fifty years or so. And *you're* Victoria Ward!' He grinned. 'I couldn't have been more wrong, could I?'

'Are you disappointed?' she asked doubtfully, hoping against all hope that he wasn't.

'Not with you. A little disappointed with myself, though, because I got things so hopelessly wrong. I'm usually right, you see. Almost always right,' he corrected with no trace of conceit. 'But what are you doing here? I shouldn't have thought that Victoria Ward ever went to parties, even if she is considerably younger than I imagined. And you're not the sort to be at a party like this.'

'Neither are you,' she almost said, and then thought better of it. 'I'm a friend of Mira's,' she explained, choosing safer ground. 'We were friends in college.'

'Who is Mira?' he asked blankly.

'Your hostess,' Victoria said pointedly. 'Joel's wife. You're supposed to be Joel's friend—at least that's what Mira said.'

'Oh, well.' He hesitated for a moment. 'I wouldn't call us friends, precisely. We knew each other once. That's all.' His expression was suddenly closed, almost remote as he turned to study the people in the crowded room.

'I thought so,' he remarked after a moment, his mood noticeably lighter as he turned back to her. 'That young woman over there—the one with the long blond hair—is about to achieve her goal.'

'What goal?' Victoria asked, following his gaze until she saw that he was looking at Linda.

'She wants to leave here with one of the unattached men.' He smiled briefly and began to search his pockets until he produced a crumpled pack of cigarettes and a surprisingly elegant gold lighter. Victoria found herself attracted by the lighter, because it didn't go with his well-worn clothes or his total lack of pretention. 'Early on, I was subjected to the full treatment, but I didn't bite, so she decided to settle on someone else. She's about to pull it off now—can you tell?'

'She can't,' Victoria said in a stricken voice, knowing full well that Linda was capable of doing exactly that.

'Of course she can. People like her do that sort of thing all the time. Why should you care? It can't matter in the least to you if she chooses to spend the night with a faceless wonder. Unless, of course, he happens to be your particular faceless wonder,' he added thoughtfully. 'But I haven't seen any signs that he is, and you don't seem the type to be attracted to faceless wonders.'

'I'm not,' she answered impatiently, watching with dismay as Linda and her young man slipped discreetly out of the apartment. 'But she was supposed to spend the weekend with me—or tonight, anyway—and now she's ruined everything.' She was fighting a rising sense of panic until she realised that he was looking expectantly down at her. There was something remarkably steadying about explaining Mira's convoluted plans to this amazing stranger.

'The logistics escape me,' he said dryly, when she was done, 'but you don't need to worry about getting home, because I'll take you.'

So he drove her home, sweeping aside her stammered objections that she lived too far out in the country, that he was supposed to spend the night with Joel and Mira, that it was an imposition for her to expect him to do this for her.

'You *don't* expect me to do this for you,' he told her, amusement colouring his voice. 'In fact, you're doing your best to talk me out of it. And I don't feel that you're imposing on me, because I don't allow people to do that.'

'Never?' she asked curiously as he steered her through the crowded room and out of the apartment.

'Never,' he answered firmly, and she believed him.

More than that, she found herself awed by the thought. She allowed so many people to impose on her—agreeing to Mira's plans for the evening being only the most recent example, she admitted ruefully. She thought wistfully that it must be marvellous to have the ability to refuse to allow people to impose on you. It was sheer force of will, she decided. Enormous willpower and enormous confidence—those were qualities this stranger had in abundance.

'I don't even know your name,' she said with surprise, breaking away from her thoughts to realise that they had left the apartment house behind. 'Mira must have told me, but I forgot.'

'It's Simon Durant, although that won't mean a thing to you. It really doesn't mean anything at all.' A brief expression of private amusement crossed his face. 'We're here,' he added, stopping mid-stride and hunting through his pockets until he found a set of keys.

Victoria looked sceptically at the car, a sleek Porsche which gleamed in the soft glow of the nearest street light. 'This is yours?' she asked in disbelief.

'I'm afraid so,' he admitted reluctantly. 'Possibly a bit ostentatious, but...' He shrugged and held the door for her.

'It does match your lighter,' she observed after he had eased himself into the driver's seat.

'You've discovered my weaknesses,' he murmured as the Porsche roared into life.

'Surely you've got more than two?'

'Perhaps.' He grinned briefly. 'We'll save them for another time. You'll have to guide me now.'

She did, directing him out of Hanover and finally on to the Interstate highway. Then, because he didn't seem disposed to talk, she kept silent, considering the unexpected kindness of fate. That seemed to be the only explanation for why such an impressive man should take an interest in her. She hadn't yet learned to refuse to allow any man to impress her; that was another lesson she'd learn bitterly, but well, thanks to Simon.

She broke her silence only to guide him from the exit to the house, and he smiled across at her after they'd pulled into the drive and he'd turned off the engine. 'You've been very understanding.'

'How?' she asked, pleased with the small compliment.

'You didn't make me feel that I had to talk to you. I like that. It comes of being a solitary soul, which is what I am.' He sounded slightly amused, as though he were sharing a private joke with her.

'I suppose I'm one, too,' she said hesitantly, not understanding his amusement.

'Of course you are,' he agreed easily, getting out of the car and coming round to open her door. 'It shows in your writing.'

But it's not the same, she wanted to tell him. You've chosen your solitary status and it pleases you. Mine has been forced upon me, and it doesn't please in the least. But she kept silent, unsure of whether she should say something quite so revealing. Besides, the atmosphere seemed to require silence.

Ahead of them, the rambling old farmhouse was dark, except for one light dimly visible through the living-room windows. Otherwise, the night was black, filled with the soft sounds of a summer breeze high among the trees. There was something magic about this night, Victoria thought, as she went slowly up the path to the front door; something magic about this man with his supreme self-confidence.

'Look how bright the stars are,' he directed as he followed her and then leaned comfortably against the rough shingled wall. 'Stars are another of my weaknesses,' he continued quietly. 'I watch the stars.

They're grand companions.' An expression of private amusement flickered across his face before he turned to look down at her.

There was an intensity in the way he was watching her which left her feeling slightly breathless. 'Would you like to come in?' she asked awkwardly. 'For a drink, or coffee?' She wished she didn't sound quite so adolescent, but she had almost never found herself on the doorstep, late at night and alone with a man—certainly never with a man like this! 'I could find something, if you like.'

'I would,' he answered deliberately, but with an engaging grin, 'if it won't make you too uncomfortable.'

'It won't,' she said firmly, surprised to realise that she meant it. In that moment, when he had recognised her awkwardness, he'd managed to dissolve it. She felt an unexpected sense of confidence and ease in his presence.

Inside the house, he decided on the wine and she went into the kitchen to get it. 'It's awfully cheap,' she apologised as she returned with the carafe and two glasses.

'That doesn't matter,' he assured her, taking the things from her. 'This place seems large for one person,' he observed as he poured for them both and then handed her one glass. 'Do you live here with your family, or is this a sort of share the rent scheme?'

'Neither.' She took one end of the couch, watching as he settled at the other, his long legs stretched out comfortably. 'I'm house-sitting for the summer. The owners are in France, and they didn't want to leave the place deserted. It's nice for me, because I get to live rent free for three months. I haven't got many expenses, so I can afford to do nothing but write. And I love being alone. After so many years of communal existence, it's grand to be by myself.'

'Has it really been so awfully long?' he asked in amusement.

'Nine years,' she told him with a weary sigh.

'Boarding school and then college.' He nodded knowingly.

'You're wrong!' She smiled across at him. 'It's reassuring to know that you *can* be, on occasion.'

'I seem to be getting a lot of things wrong about you. That isn't like me. You look like a boarding school and college kind of girl,' he told her almost reproachfully. 'What have you been doing of a communal nature since you were——' he calculated rapidly '—thirteen?'

'You're right about college. That's been the last four years, living in dorms with roommates. During the summers, I've been working at a resort. You get to live in what amounts to a barracks.'

'And before that?' he prompted gently.

'I was in Florida,' she answered, 'with my uncle and aunt and their four children. It tended to be a little crowded. My parents died when I was thirteen, you see,' she continued more easily than she would have thought possible. Usually she hated the moment when she had to explain this to someone, always afraid that she would come off sounding slightly pathetic. But for reasons she didn't quite understand, she didn't have this fear now. 'They died in an automobile accident,' she finished simply.

'No brothers or sisters?' he asked, and she was pleased that nothing in his voice suggested pity.

'No. The only family I had was Daddy's brother and *his* family. I had to go and live with them. It's just as well that I was an only child. With me added to their four, there wasn't much room.' She smiled, because long ago she'd made the decision that no one should ever know just how awkward and lonely those years had been. 'It wasn't easy for them, and it was good of them to have me.'

'But you waited until you could leave, and stop being a burden to them.' He nodded with understanding.

'How did you know that?'

'One of my correct assumptions,' he explained with a grin, setting down his glass long enough to find his cigarettes. 'Strange,' he continued, after he had one lit, 'I wouldn't have taken you for an orphan, but I suppose you are. That goes a long way towards explaining a few things about you, I think.'

'What kind of things?'

'How a twenty-two year old girl can manage to be Victoria Ward. I could tell, just from looking at you at the party, that you had a certain serenity and wisdom. But I'd never have taken you for Victoria Ward.'

'Because she's seventy, if she's a day,' Victoria supplied.

'Because people don't acquire that kind of serenity and wisdom until they're about seventy. Well, most people don't acquire it at all,' he qualified, 'but, if they do, it comes with age. It's acceptance. Not quite resignation, but a considerable degree of acceptance and patience.' He nodded thoughtfully. 'It also makes me understand just what it was that appealed to me, when I read those two little stories of yours.'

'What?' she asked quickly, not sure she was following him completely, but entranced all the same.

'We've got a surprising similarity,' he explained, leaning forward to stub out his cigarette and then pour himself more wine. 'You see,' he continued after a moment, 'I'm an orphan, too, although it's probably stretching the point to consider myself an orphan at my age. But the feelings don't go away just because you've reached an age where both your parents might have died in the natural course of events. Mine didn't, though, and I suppose one never stops feeling like an orphan.' He hesitated for a moment and then went through the business of lighting another cigarette.

'But that's the only similarity between us,' he resumed, studying his cigarette with great absorption. 'You had a certain degree of continuity and stability for thirteen years, while I've had none. I haven't even got the least idea of what my name ought to be. Nor have I any idea of what my parents' names actually were. I haven't got a name.' He smiled, a brief, wintry smile.

'But you have,' Victoria said softly. 'You told me it. I think Simon Durant is a name that has considerable distinction.'

'It hasn't anything at all.' He sipped his wine slowly and then leaned back, closing his eyes. 'It's a fabrication—absolutely meaningless. My mother took particular pains to make that clear to me, before she died.'

'And when was that?' Victoria asked carefully, sensing that he expected some response from her.

'When I was five. She wanted me to understand that I'd never had a father in any acceptable sense of that word. And, while she'd known his name, she hadn't given it to me. Nor had she given me her own. She'd made one up out of whole cloth—that was her expression. She liked the name. That was all.'

'What an extraordinary thing to tell a five-year-old,' Victoria whispered.

'I expect she was an extraordinary woman, in her fashion. I don't remember her very well, of course, but that's the impression I have. And I can't think why I've told you any of this,' he said with an abrupt change of mood, suddenly uncomfortable. 'Perhaps it's because it's so very late—or so very early. I'm not sure which.'

Victoria followed his glance towards the windows and saw the light of dawn beginning to streak the sky.

'It's midsummer's night, you know,' he said with a humourless smile. 'The shortest night of the year. You'd think I could have held my tongue on the shortest night of the year. I had no business telling you about myself. I don't tell anyone about this. I never have. God knows why I've told you, except——' He stopped, his eyes holding hers.

She knew what was going to happen, even before he leaned towards her and bent his head. His lips found hers with a curious gentleness, but she sensed the need or hunger he was holding in check. She wanted to wrap her arms around him and pull him close, allow him to destroy his self-control and her own. But the moment was too fragile for that; for both of them, this was too new and unexpected. She was afraid of what might happen if they upset the delicate balance of what they felt for each other. Later, of course, she would realise just how right she had been to be afraid. She would learn that it was best to allow no one to upset the delicate balance of her life. But all of that was far from her mind at this moment as the kiss ended and he pulled away from her.

'Have I insulted you?' he asked carefully.

'No.'

'That surprises me—but then, you've been surprising me since the moment I met you. I've been surprising myself, too. But now I think I'd better go, before I make things any worse than they already are.'

'No,' Victoria said without thinking, terrified that he might leave. If he left, he'd never come back. She knew that instinctively, and she couldn't bear the thought of never seeing him again. There was no way she could know what a dreadful mistake she was making, how much wiser it would have been to let him walk out of her life that first night. 'You can't leave now,' she protested. 'If you do, you'll decide that you shouldn't have told me, and you'll never tell anyone else.'

'And why should that matter to you?' he asked without expression.

'I don't want that,' she tried to explain. 'I don't want you to be alone with it.'

'I don't either—not right now,' he admitted reluctantly.

'Then you can have the couch,' she told him briskly, getting to her feet. 'Finish your wine while I get you a blanket.'

She left the room without a backward glance, running lightly up the stairs to pull a quilt and a pillow from the guest room bed. She could as easily have given him the room, but she sensed that it was better not to. This moment demanded a certain distance, not the intimacy of going up the stairs together.

When she returned to the living room, he took the quilt from her and then hesitated, appearing confused or uncertain. 'I don't think you should be doing this,' he said with a forced smile. 'You're much too nice to associate with a bastard like me.'

'Don't ever use that word again!' she told him sharply, surprising them both with her vehemence. Then, without saying anything more, she turned and ran lightly up the two flights of stairs to the room she was using at the top of the house. She closed her door and leaned against it, feeling suddenly breathless. The breathlessness had nothing to do with the two flights of stairs, and a great deal to do with the fact that Simon Durant was staying for what remained of the night.

It seemed a glorious moment in her life. She had found someone who mattered to her as no one had since her parents had died. Even more glorious was the apparent evidence that she actually mattered to this marvellous, almost mystical man. It seemed so long since she had really mattered to anyone, even herself. She felt a sudden rush of gratitude to Simon for the precious gift he had given her.

CHAPTER THREE

THUS had the possession begun. It was only later, with the perspective of time and a hard-won objectivity, that Victoria was able to see it for what it had been. She had allowed herself to be possessed by Simon, fascinated and dazzled by his extraordinary self-confidence with the hint of vulnerability beneath. She had been pathetically anxious to love him and be loved by him, to be done with the years of loneliness and isolation.

She had never allowed these feelings to surface until she met Simon. She hadn't dared to love anyone, had lacked the courage to trust anyone that much. Nor had she believed that anyone could love her. She thought that love had left her life when her parents had died. But Simon had seemed different, had seemed to have enough courage for both of them. She trusted him without question—the only time she'd been fool enough to trust anyone. She had thought him her knight-errant. He had come to her defence at the party, he had enveloped her in the comforting warmth of his regard and admiration for her. He had trusted her enough to tell her what he had never told anyone else. How could she not trust him in return?

She had loved him with a passionate absorption born of thirteen years of isolation. She had loved him because he was calm and sure, devastatingly attractive, and because there was a quality about him which made him larger than life. Most of all, she had loved him because—in some strange way she didn't quite understand—he seemed to need her as much as she knew she needed him.

These feelings grew and intensified during the next day, a perfect day without a cloud in the sky and the air already hot but tempered by a light breeze. They had packed a picnic lunch and set out to explore the back roads and quiet towns in the area.

Simon had announced that he wanted to see the settings of her two stories. 'I know they're real places,' he had told her with a quick grin. 'It's another of my correct assumptions about you.'

It was his decision to save the old graveyard, the setting of her first story, until they were ready for lunch. 'It seems like the perfect place to have a picnic,' he explained, 'unless you think it's sacrilegious to have a picnic in a graveyard.'

'I hope it isn't,' she admitted, 'because I've often done it.'

'I rather thought you had.' He looked pleased, and even more so when they reached the spot. 'Very nice,' he said briefly as he surveyed the scene.

They were at the end of a narrow dirt road, the nearest house almost a mile away. Behind a wrought iron fence, the gravestones were in no particular order, a few settled at odd angles. The ground rose gently and then levelled out where an ancient maple tree provided a pool of shade against the summer sun.

'Why aren't you married?' Simon asked when they had finished their lunch, sweeping aside the remains and settling himself more comfortably. 'You look like the sort of girl who would be.'

'I haven't wanted to be,' she answered without thinking, her tone sharper than she would have wished. She trusted Simon, but she didn't want to explain that, until this moment, she'd never had the courage to allow herself to love anyone.

'Haven't you?' he asked with a slow smile, his eyes holding hers as though he were reading her thoughts.

'But surely there have been legions of willing young men?'

'Hardly legions,' she protested, beginning to blush. 'There was only one who actually got to the point of saying, "Vicky, will you marry me?" But he really doesn't count, because we didn't know each other as well as he thought we did.'

'You must not have known each other well at all—not if he actually had to ask you to marry him. Not that I'm an expert at the business—God knows I'm not,' he added parenthetically, 'but I think that two people who love each other enough to marry already know it's going to happen, without either of them having to ask.'

'Perhaps,' she agreed carefully. That, of course, was how he would do it, if he decided to marry someone.

'And there's the problem of someone calling you Vicky,' he continued thoughtfully. 'You're not a Vicky—there's no depth or composure to a Vicky. *You* have both to a remarkable extent. You're quite right—he didn't know you well enough. I'm glad you turned him down.' He favoured her with another slow smile, his eyes holding hers.

She looked away, wondering a little wildly just how much she ought to read into his last statement. It seemed logical to assume that he was glad she'd turned down someone else because he wanted her for himself. Yet he really hadn't given her any cause to reach that conclusion. He might admire her and trust her enough to tell her something he'd never told anyone else, but that didn't necessarily mean that he loved her and wanted to marry her. She was allowing herself to imagine entirely too much, she told herself firmly, wishing that the thought didn't make her feel quite so unhappy.

'This is a peaceful spot,' Simon observed after a moment, and she suspected that he was deliberately changing the subject. 'Some people don't like graveyards, but I find this one comforting. No one likes death, but what I object to are untimely deaths—violent ones, ones for no reason. But this place doesn't have the feeling of untimely death about it,' he continued, leaning forward to study the closest tombstone. 'Nothing untimely about this, is there?' he asked and then read aloud from the inscription on the stone. '"Here lies interred ye remains of Mrs Susanna Rawson, wife of ye Reverend William Rawson. Died May ye sixteenth, 1748, in ye seventy-second year of her age."' He pushed aside the grass growing around the base of the stone, so that he could see the epitaph carved there. '"The heart of her husband safely trusted in her." Now there's a thought,' he mused, still looking at the stone. 'I wonder how it feels to safely trust another person. I've never been much good at trusting people. I've got too many defences in place to allow myself to trust anyone. It's inevitable, I suppose, given the life I've led.' He turned back to her, studying her face with a puzzled frown. 'But I think you could do it, if anybody could.'

'Do what?' she asked carefully.

'Destroy my defences,' he answered promptly. 'I've got a lot of them, you know, but you've already destroyed quite a few.'

'Have I?'

'Of course you have. They've been falling like so many tenpins, almost since the moment I met you. I might find that I could safely trust in you. I wonder why.' Suddenly he leaned across the distance separating them. 'You are quite enchanting,' he whispered, his lips against her forehead.

'Am I really?' she asked, thinking that this was a dream come true as her hands came to rest on his shoulders.

'Of course you are.' There was laughter in his voice. 'Everything about you is enchanting,' he breathed, beginning to run his fingers slowly through her long hair. 'I've been wanting to do this since the moment I met you. It tangles so delightfully. I love it.'

'I don't think you're being serious,' she protested weakly, completely under the spell of his touch.

'But I am, dear girl,' he said softly. 'I've never been more serious in my life. In fact, I am perilously close to having my last defence destroyed—because of you.' He kissed her carefully, his lips lingering for an endless moment on hers. Then he folded her into his arms, resting her head against his shoulder.

'And I'm not minding it at all,' he continued lazily. 'I've always assumed that I'd bitterly resent anyone who managed to upset the delicate balance of my life. But here I am, allowing you to do just that—not twenty-four hours after we meet—and I'm actually enjoying it enormously.' He pulled her even closer, holding her against him in a curiously protective gesture. There didn't seem to be any need for words, she thought contentedly. She was in his arms and willing to let the moment go on forever. She closed her eyes, wondering if she'd ever been as happy as she was now.

'You know,' he finally said, disturbing their companionable silence, 'this is romantic, but hardly comfortable. You've got to let me stretch my legs while there's still some circulation left in them.'

Obligingly, she moved away, watching with amusement as he slowly straightened his legs. 'I'm too old for this sort of activity,' he complained, stretching out full length across the blanket. He crossed his arms under his head and looked reproachfully up at her. 'You're not stiff at all, because you're so young. I ought to have done this a good ten years ago—possibly even fifteen—before my joints began to stiffen up on me.'

'You make yourself sound positively ancient,' she protested.

'I feel positively ancient.' He sighed and closed his eyes.

'How old are you?'

'Much too old for you,' he answered, sounding less than pleased to admit that fact.

'You don't look it.'

He opened his eyes long enough to give her a sceptical glance.

'Well, perhaps a little worn at the edges,' she conceded, noting the fine lines around his eyes.

'More than a little,' he murmured.

'But that's not because you're old.' She hesitated for a moment. 'Would you mind if I asked you a question?'

'You may ask me any number of them,' he said cheerfully. 'I may not answer them, of course, but there's no harm in asking.'

'That's what I thought.' She nodded gravely and then gathered her courage. 'What do you do?'

'A great many things,' he answered easily. 'I knew you'd ask that one, but what I do isn't worth discussing.'

'Still, it must pay well,' she observed, glancing involuntarily down the hill to where the gleaming Porsche was parked. 'Perhaps you're a gangster, growing rich from a life of crime.'

'I don't believe I qualify,' he said apologetically.

'No, I didn't think you did. You don't look like a criminal, for one thing. You spend too much time outdoors for one.'

'Do I?' he asked with an enigmatic smile.

'Yes, you do,' she answered positively. 'Where are you from? And I'm only asking because I can hear a bit of an accent, although I don't know what it is.'

SAFELY TO TRUST

'I was born in New York,' he began dispassionately, 'but we were living in California when my mother died. After that, I lived in foster homes—first in California and then in Texas for a few more years. Since then I've been on the move almost constantly. We haven't time for me to tell you all the places I've been—even if I could remember them all, which I seriously doubt.' There was a sudden hint of reserve in his tone, and she realised that he wasn't about to allow her to carry this discussion of his life any further. 'What about you?' he asked after a moment, deliberately changing the subject. 'You're only twenty-two. What do you plan to do with the rest of your life?'

'I can't possibly know what I'm going to do with all of it,' she pointed out reasonably, prepared to follow him to this safer topic. 'But I graduated from Dartmouth last month, and I start work in the fall. I'll be a reporter.'

'And what will you report?' he asked idly.

'Whatever there is to report. I've got a job with Global News Service, in the New Hampshire bureau. They really *do* have a New Hampshire bureau,' she assured him as she saw his sceptical glance. 'But that's just a start. I mean to do well, so they'll advance me and send me to other places. I want to travel and *do* things. As you have,' she finished with a burst of emotion.

'And how do you know that about me?' he asked lazily, his eyes closed against the sun.

'I can tell some things about you, and I can guess others,' she attempted to explain. 'I think you've been to a lot of strange places, and you've done challenging things. It's as though you test yourself, or try to prove yourself. Last night, I had the thought that you must climb mountains or hack your way through jungles.'

'You don't hack your way through a jungle,' he

objected, grinning. 'That's the wrong way to go about a jungle. You've seen too many bad movies.'

'How do you get through a jungle?' she asked, interested by this sudden bit of revelation.

'Very carefully. You don't fight a jungle, if you're wise. You accept it and learn to use it. Jungles are very subtle things, and it's best to approach them with equal subtlety. One does much better that way. And that's your lesson on jungles for today,' he finished with an apologetic smile.

'Have you spent a lot of time in jungles?'

'Yes,' he answered briefly, a faraway look in his eyes. 'I wonder why I told you that,' he mused after a moment, deliberately attempting to shake off his mood. 'You're an insidious little thing—do you know that? Destroying my defences, making me say things I don't intend to say.'

'I don't *make* you say anything,' she protested.

'Of course you do.' With one swift movement, he pulled her down beside him and touched her face, his fingers lingering, warm against her skin. 'Or make me want to. Make me want *you*,' he corrected just before his lips found hers.

Just as she wanted him, she thought distractedly as his mouth moved slowly over hers. He was demanding more of a response from her than she'd ever felt before, ever imagined possible. His hands were confident against her back, moulding her body into his while her need for him grew stronger. She slipped her arms around his neck, moving even closer as she returned his kiss with equal passion.

'You make it almost too difficult to resist,' he whispered as his lips finally left hers and came to rest on the hollow at the base of her throat. 'Nearly impossible, in fact.'

'I don't want you to,' she confessed as his hands

began to trace each line and curve of her body with infinite care. She came alive to his touch and stirred restlessly against him as he found new and marvellous ways to excite her.

'Does anyone ever come here?' he asked unevenly, his fingers beginning to work at the buttons of her dress.

'Never,' she whispered, her thoughts spinning dizzily as he pushed her dress away. She sighed as his fingers began to run in lazy circles on her skin, brushing lightly against her breasts and lingering there. His mouth found hers again, parting her lips with expert passion. She was lost in a world of sensation, clinging helplessly to him, wanting the firm line of his body against hers.

Her fingers fumbled with the buttons of his shirt. She needed more of him; she couldn't help herself as desire overwhelmed her. It was all so new; she was frightened by the intensity of her need to be possessed by him. But her need was greater than her fear as she pulled his shirt away and felt the hard muscled strength of his body beneath her hands.

She heard his quick, indrawn breath, felt his lips trailing softly across her skin as they followed his hands. 'Darling girl,' he murmured. 'I love you so.'

'I love you, too,' she breathed. 'My knight-errant.' She smiled up at him, overcome by a wave of tenderness. 'That's what I thought you were, the first time I saw you.'

'And so I should like to be,' he agreed, an odd catch in his voice. He was suddenly motionless and then she felt him carefully easing away from her. 'You shouldn't have told me,' he said unsteadily as he turned on his side and gently pulled her into a very different sort of embrace. 'But it's just as well that you did.'

'Why?' she asked, feeling cold and empty as he automatically began to pull her dress together and fasten the buttons.

'Because I should like to be your knight-errant,' he said with an attempt at a smile. 'I shouldn't have let things go so far. We were getting entirely too carried away—a foolish thing to do.'

'But I want to be carried away,' she protested. 'What are you doing? Trying to get all your defences back in place? You don't need them and I don't want them.' She reached out to touch his face, but he moved away from her, sitting up and locking his hands around his knees.

'This has nothing to do with my defences, darling girl,' he said with a grin, searching his pockets until he found his cigarettes and then taking a moment to light one. 'It does, however, have a great deal to do with yours. Or rather——' he paused to smile again, '—with your lack of them right now.'

'I don't know what you mean.' She stirred resentfully and then pushed herself up beside him.

'I don't expect you do.' He studied the glowing tip of his cigarette for a moment and then turned to look at her. 'Tell me one thing. Have you ever wanted——' he smiled disarmingly. 'Have you ever wanted to be carried away before?'

She shook her head, uncomfortably aware that she was blushing.

'I thought not. I was afraid not,' he amended. 'As pleasant as it might be, I'm disinclined to take advantage of someone quite as innocent as you. What you need, I think, is a little time for sober reflection.' He paused to study her face. 'You don't want sober reflection—that's obvious.'

'Not any more,' she said defiantly.

'Good Lord! You're not making this any easier.' He smiled abstractedly. 'You might at least allow me the luxury of being honourable. Darling girl, we'd create all sorts of problems for ourselves, if we did what we'd both like to do right now! You'd be overcome with guilt,' he pointed out reasonably. 'In the long run, you're simply not the sort of girl to do this kind of thing. Even if you were,' he hurried on as she began to object, 'I'd feel I had to make an honest woman of you.'

'Are you really that old-fashioned?' she asked looking curiously up at him.

'Not as a general rule. Perhaps you stimulate whatever old-fashioned instincts I have.' He hesitated for an instant. 'I'm suddenly remembering that my father saw no need to make an honest woman of my mother. I'm determined not to do the same to you. If I'm to do this thing, I'd like to do it properly.' Then he effectively ended the moment by getting to his feet and beginning to gather up the remains of their lunch.

Only in retrospect did Victoria see that the pattern of their brief relationship had been established that afternoon. Simon had allowed himself to go only just so far before withdrawing. He had talked about trust, but he hadn't trusted her completely. And she had been so desperately anxious for his love that she hadn't possessed a shred of pride. She had been prepared to do anything and sacrifice everything when he withdrew. That afternoon, she had come perilously close to begging him to make love to her; later she would go even further and humiliate herself to an even greater extent. It was as though she considered her body to be a form of payment, with which she could buy his love. But none of that had become obvious until long after he had left her.

That evening, back at the house, things had started promisingly enough. Simon announced that he would make their dinner and proceeded to do so as Victoria watched. He raided the refrigerator and the cupboards with cheerful abandon, using nearly all the cooking pans and leaving the counter space strewn with debris. Ultimately, he produced what he assured her was curry.

'It doesn't look like any curry I've ever had,' she said doubtfully, staring down at her plate.

'You'll like it,' he assured her as he poured the wine. 'I'm a wonderful cook. I've managed to make rat palatable—or at least bearable. I can't miss when I've got better stuff to work with.'

'Have you really eaten a rat?' she asked, appalled at the thought.

'More than one, actually, but only when I had to. I've no great fondness for rat, believe me.'

'Why did you have to do it?'

'There wasn't anything else,' he answered briefly.

'Was this when you were in the jungle?' she persisted, refusing to hear the warning in his voice.

'Yes.' He nodded impatiently. 'That's one of the problems we've got to face. My life—which has been a great deal different from yours—keeps intruding.'

'Why is that a problem?' she asked uneasily.

'Because we're so different,' he answered, his voice tightly controlled. 'I can't imagine two more different people. I really don't know anything about the sort of world you live in, and you couldn't begin to understand the kind of life I've been living. I wouldn't want you to.' Without another word, he began to eat, the continuing silence hanging heavy over the table.

Uneasily, Victoria picked at her food. The silence lengthened, with Simon obviously caught by a mood which left him isolated and remote. He was dwelling on the kind of life he'd been living; she was sure of that and the thought filled her with foreboding. She had imagined his life to be one of high adventure, but now she realised that it was something very different, something darker. Instinctively, she knew that it threatened their relationship, and the thought terrified her.

When they were done with the pretence of eating, she began to clear the table while Simon lit a cigarette and then wandered into the living room. She wavered uncertainly for a moment and then followed him. He was sitting on the couch, looking out of the west window to watch the last of the setting sun.

'You're going to leave, aren't you?' she finally asked, unable to avoid facing the truth any longer.

'What makes you think that?' He turned to face her, his features hidden by the shadows.

'I don't know.' She shrugged as she came to sit down beside him, beginning to nervously finger his lighter which lay just in front of her on the coffee table. 'There are things I know about you without being told,' she tried to explain. 'I just sense them—as though they're waiting somewhere in my mind—and then they come to the surface and I can *see* them. Right now I can see that you're going to leave,' she finished miserably.

'And do you see fame and fortune, and a beautiful dark-haired woman in my future?' he asked, stubbing out his cigarette and then drawing her into his arms. 'Be serious, dear girl!' He looked down at her, his black mood suddenly gone. 'You sound like a second-rate fortune teller who has lost her crystal ball.'

'I don't care,' she whispered helplessly, trying to maintain coherence as his lips began to tease the corner of her mouth. Then she didn't care at all as his mouth closed over hers and his hands grew bolder. She surrendered completely, wanting physical sensation to drive away her fears. Almost desperately, she strained against his touch while his kisses deepened and grew more insistent.

'This is marvellous,' he breathed when his lips had moved on to find the valley between her breasts.

'Nothing frightens me when we're like this.' Then he sighed. 'But this has nothing to do with trust. That's the problem.' Abruptly, he raised his head.

'This *is* trust,' she said with fierce intensity.

'Not the sort of trust I mean,' he explained as he carefully released her. 'This is the sort of thing that could happen with any woman, but you're not just any woman. I need time, Victoria,' he continued uneasily. 'I don't know about love. I don't understand it. It's new to me, and not entirely comfortable. There's an element of self-protection working, too,' he continued after a pause. 'I've made a point of never trusting anyone but myself, but this won't work for us if I can't trust you.'

'You *can* trust me,' she urged.

'That's easy enough for you to say,' he complained almost irritably, 'but hard for me to accept. All the same, I *do* love you,' he finished with sudden conviction. 'I *will* come back. We'll leave it at that, for now.' Slowly he got to his feet.

'No,' she protested, staring up at him with haunted eyes. 'You can't leave me now.'

'It's as good a time as any,' he said dispassionately. 'There's no point in prolonging things.'

'No!' She stood up and slipped her arms around him, pulling her body against his with wild and thoughtless longing. 'Please stay a while,' she whispered helplessly. 'Stay the night.'

'I want to,' he told her very gently, understanding exactly what she meant. 'But not if I can't love you as I should.'

'You do,' she sighed, her fingers tracing the muscles of his back. 'I know you do.'

'Only with reservation, darling girl,' he said with difficulty. 'Give me a chance to work things through.' Abruptly, he wrapped his arms around her, moulding her body even closer to his as he kissed her with an urgency quite unlike anything before.

'And that will have to do for now.' His voice was unsteady as he finally released her. 'I'll think about you—you can be sure of that. Almost constantly, I expect.' He grinned briefly. 'And I *will* come back. I promise you that.' Then, before she could say anything, he was gone.

CHAPTER FOUR

VICTORIA hadn't believed him. She had spent too many years knowing that she must not believe in anyone, knowing that her life would always be one of lonely isolation. It seemed impossible to believe that things might change, that Simon would come back and change them for her. In the years ahead, she would find black humour in the fact that she had been only half wrong. Simon had come back to her, but his coming had changed nothing except her view of the world and her resolve never to believe in anyone again.

He came in the early morning, just as dawn was streaking the sky. She awoke to hear the distant sound of his knock on the door. She knew it was Simon, and she didn't bother with her robe or slippers as she raced down the stairs to open the door for him. He was nothing but a vague shadow against the darker shadows outside, tall and lean and reassuringly there. When she drew him into the hall and switched on the light so she could see him properly, he closed his eyes against the sudden brightness. Victoria took those few moments to study his face. It seemed drawn and thinner, as though he had lost weight or been under a great strain, or possibly both. 'Are you all right?' she asked uncertainly.

'I expect so. I haven't given it much thought.' He attempted a smile. 'I feel as though I've been travelling for days. I don't sleep on planes, and I'm fighting an extreme case of jet lag, with some culture shock thrown in for good measure. How long was I gone?' he asked unexpectedly.

'Just about a month,' she said without emotion, as

though that month hadn't seemed like years. 'You look as though you need some food, and then a proper bed. I can give you both,' she suggested, smiling up at him.

He shook his head impatiently. 'Just a shower—a good hot one—and then a change of clothes. I'll be more coherent after that.' He stepped back to the door and retrieved a flight bag from the step. 'If you could tell me where to go,' he finished abruptly.

'There's a guest room at the top of the stairs, and the bathroom is next to it,' she told him, swallowing her disappointment at his brusqueness.

He nodded. 'I'll be down as soon as I'm done. Then we have to talk,' he finished ominously as he started up the stairs.

Victoria waited in the hall, listening as he moved slowly around the guest room and then went into the bathroom, closing the door behind him. When she heard the shower running, she went silently up the stairs and into his room. It gave her comfort to see his things: the open flight bag, the crumpled pile of clothes, the contents of his pockets on the bureau.

She needed that comfort right now. She hadn't liked the way he'd said they had to talk. She had the feeling that talking would lead to unpleasant facts, things she didn't want to face. Besides, she didn't want to talk, she thought with a flash of defiance. She only wanted to be with Simon and let him fill the emptiness she'd lived through during this last month.

'What are you doing here?'

She turned at the sound of his voice, not having heard him come into the room, and drew a quick breath at the sight of him. His hair was still damp from the shower and he was wearing a white towelling robe, tied loosely at the waist. Involuntarily, her eyes were drawn to the broad expanse of his chest, visible where the robe was parted.

'I couldn't bear to just wait downstairs,' she explained hesitantly, very much aware of his sheer masculine power and of the potential intimacy of the moment.

'You might have waited until I had some clothes on.' There was a gleam of amusement in his eyes as he came towards her. 'And put on a few more, yourself.'

'I didn't think of that,' she whispered shyly, wondering if that really were the truth.

'No?' he asked sceptically, his hands brushing lightly against the thin fabric of her nightgown as he pulled her into his arms. 'I'm not sure I believe you.' His lips traced the curve of her cheek and then lingered at the base of her throat. 'But I'm glad you came.'

'Are you?' she asked dreamily, distracted by the touch of his lips on her skin and the way his hands were moving slowly up and down her back. She leaned gratefully against him as he pulled her closer, tentatively allowing her hands to rest against the rough fabric of his robe.

'I've never come back to anyone before,' he said, sounding a little distracted himself as he lifted his head to study her face. Then his mouth closed over hers with slow deliberation, exploring gently while she clung helplessly to him.

She hadn't known how much she'd longed for this, how deep had been her need. He was driving the month of loneliness away as his mouth possessed hers and his hands traced the curves of her body, moulding her against him. She slipped her arms around his neck as she gave herself completely to his embrace.

'I wanted to come back to you,' he breathed when his lips had moved on, teasing her skin with their touch, exploring the soft swell of her breasts just above the low neckline of her gown. 'I wanted you so much.'

'I wanted you, too,' she admitted helplessly as his

mouth grew more insistent and his hands continued their soft caresses. The thin fabric of her gown was no real barrier as he found her breasts and stroked them gently.

'You know I care, don't you?' he murmured, and she nodded slowly, completely under his spell. 'I care so much,' he added just before his mouth claimed hers again.

This time his kiss teased lightly, a distracting contrast to his hands which had suddenly grown bolder. They were exploring her body freely, brushing away the straps of her nightgown and moving down, warm against her skin. She felt the gown fall away and there was nothing left to separate his touch from her body. He caressed her with infinite tenderness while desire stirred within her and she strained against his touch, longing for possession. She clung helplessly to him as his fingers began to move in slow and lazy circles of delight, flickering like fire against her skin.

She was drawn even deeper into this new world as his lips left hers, tracing the curve of her breast and leaving her breathless with desire. Her hands touched his hair and then moved slowly down to slip beneath his robe and feel the hard muscled strength of his chest. Sensation overwhelmed her as she explored his body, her passion meeting his. Mindlessly, she drifted on the tide, clinging to him as he laid her gently on the bed and joined her there.

'I've been afraid,' he murmured, gathering her into his arms. 'I thought I'd left you for too long.'

'You almost did,' she agreed absently, pushing away his robe so that she could complete their closeness. Now that they were together, she didn't care about the past, could hardly remember it.

It seemed that time was standing still as they savoured their closeness. The first passion had been replaced by deliberate tenderness and the desire to prolong this moment of discovery. They moved lazily against each other, his lips against her hair while she ran her hands across his shoulders and then his arms. She hesitated when she felt a jagged line of flesh. 'What's this?' she asked, exploring it with her fingers.

'Never mind.' He shifted slightly, moving his arm away.

'Is it a scar?' She reached out to touch it again.

'I suppose it must be,' he answered with a hint of reserve.

'How did it happen?' she persisted. 'I want to know the things that have happened to you.'

'Too many things have happened to me,' he said, his face closed and his body suddenly rigid against hers. 'All things I wish I didn't have to tell you—things you'll despise.' Abruptly, he pulled away from her, sitting up and slipping into his robe while he avoided her eyes.

'That's not true,' she protested, sitting up and then hastily gathering the sheet around her. 'Nothing will change how I feel about you.'

'That's adolescent fancy.' His voice was bitter. 'Easy to say, before you know the truth. I'm not what you think I am,' he continued almost savagely. 'You've got some romantic notion of me as a knight-errant, and I'm anything but that. There's nothing noble about my life. I've spent too much if it considering how to most effectively take other people's lives.'

'What are you talking about?' she demanded, trying to make sense of his words.

'I've lived off war,' he said abruptly. 'I've been drawn to war, fascinated by it. I've actually enjoyed it,' he added with distaste.

'I don't believe you,' she whispered, desperately trying to break through this sudden wall he'd built between them.

'But it's true,' he said irritably. 'It's what I've done with my life. Wars have the advantage of being nothing but distance and the rejection of any contact. That's what I've wanted. I've used isolation like a crutch, and it has served me very well.'

Until now, she wanted to say, but kept silent because she didn't think he would hear her. He was talking rapidly, pouring out the story of his life. She couldn't comprehend what he was saying and she caught only fragments of it all.

He was telling her about his schooling and about enlisting in the army, explaining more than she could understand about such things as Ranger training and a jungle tracking school. It was about guerilla warfare, first in the army and then later, on his own. He told her that he'd become adept at making contacts and offering his services—whatever that means, she thought a little wildly, her mind racing as it attempted to keep up with his words, if not their meaning.

'I didn't concern myself with right or wrong,' he was saying. 'I simply wanted to be a part of it, where no one cares that I'm a bastard without a name. All that has mattered is that I know what I'm doing and do it very well.

'But I suddenly hate the thought of it—the way I've used so many people to meet my own needs. It wasn't until I met you that I realised there might be something else.' For the first time since his recital had started, he acknowledged her presence by reaching for her hand. 'But you see,' he continued with difficulty, 'I don't know if that will last. What if I stop hating it? Even if I don't, how long will it be until you decide that you don't like what I am any better than I do?'

'But that won't happen,' she said firmly, overcome by a fierce rush of emotion. While she didn't fully understand what he had been telling her, she knew she loved him even more than ever, with a fierce protectiveness that left her shaken. She pulled her hand free and touched his unyielding back, slipping her arms around his neck and leaning close to him. 'I'll never love you any less,' she breathed, touching her lips to his shoulder and allowing her hands to brush lightly against his chest. 'I'll love you more, because I know you need me.' She pulled him even closer, resting her head on his shoulder. 'I didn't think you needed me, and I needed you so much. You've given me so much,' she finished, wondering if she'd managed to reach him.

'What have I given you?' he asked reluctantly, as though he wanted to believe but didn't dare trust himself to do so.

'You've made me feel safe,' she tried to explain. 'You've been someone I could love, and you wanted me when no one else did. It's been years since anyone has wanted me, or since I've mattered to anyone. That all stopped when my parents died. But *you* wanted me, and I *mattered* to you,' she finished, clinging helplessly to him, no longer sure where her need left off and his began.

'Is that what you felt?' he asked, sounding shaken. She felt the tension leaving his body as he turned and drew her into his arms. 'I didn't know. I saw your strength and your composure, and I didn't think I was giving you anything in return.'

'You were giving me everything,' she whispered, possessed by a wild hunger as her hands moved restlessly against him. 'I wanted to be able to give you something back.'

'You've done that,' he murmured, pulling her closer. 'You've made me believe. I don't know how, but you've done it.' His lips lost themselves in the valley between her breasts while he caressed her, his touch like fire against her skin. 'We've been such fools,' he whispered.

'Such fools.' From a great distance, she heard his sigh. 'And we're about to be even greater fools,' he said roughly, his touch suddenly withdrawn.

'No,' she protested mindlessly, craving the heat of his body while her mouth hungrily tasted his skin. 'Don't leave me now,' she begged, beyond control.

'It's too soon,' he said gently, pulling away from her.

'It's not.' She stared up at him with bewildered eyes as he began to draw the sheet over her. 'Please,' she pleaded, reaching out to touch him. 'It's not too soon.'

'But it is. I nearly forgot that.' His hands captured hers, imprisoning them in his grasp. 'Darling Victoria, don't make it any harder. It's hard enough as it is.'

'But it doesn't have to be,' she breathed, still possessed by her aching need for him. 'I want you so.'

'I'm well aware of that,' he agreed, and she hated him for his control. 'But I can't do that to you.'

'You can,' she cried. 'I want you to! I need you, Simon. Please?' she begged, dying inside as he pulled away. 'I want you to love me now,' she finished, looking up at him with haunted eyes.

'Not yet.' He hesitated for an instant. 'I can't let myself do what my father did.'

'I don't care what your father did!'

'But *I* do,' he told her gently. 'Don't you see? This is something we can't do until you're my wife.'

'And perhaps I never will be,' she flared, pain and emptiness tearing her apart. Now, when she needed him most, when she'd offered herself to him without any vestige of pride, when she'd begged him to love her, he'd turned her away. 'Perhaps you don't intend to marry me! Is this more of not letting anyone into your life?' she demanded bitterly. 'Of using isolation like a crutch?' Shaking with anger, she flung his words back at him.

'It's none of that,' he said evenly, but she knew she'd

struck a nerve. 'It's wanting—for once in my life—to do things differently.'

'It's not doing things differently,' she raged. 'It's doing what you've always done, only this time you're doing it to me.'

'For God's sake, Victoria,' he snapped 'try to understand! It's because I love you that I'm doing this. Until we're married——'

'Then marry me now,' she begged, and hated herself for her weakness.

'But I can't,' he said, while she refused to hear the anguish in his voice. 'There isn't time. I shouldn't even have taken the time to come back to you, but I had to. I have to leave again, today.' He touched her hand in a mute gesture of appeal. 'I had to come back long enough to get things settled.'

'You call this settled?' she demanded bitterly. 'To come back only long enough to tell me that you're leaving again?'

'Victoria, I have a commitment—something I have to do—and the worst of it is that I can't explain it to you.' He sighed wearily. 'But it's the last one—I promise you that.'

'Until the next time,' she said flatly.

'Victoria,' he began more gently, 'there isn't going to be a next time. There wouldn't even be this time, if I hadn't given my word. I have to keep it. It's simply——'

'There's nothing simple about it,' she raged, refusing to let him finish. 'It could be simple; it would be for anyone else. But you want to make it as complicated as possible. You're only toying with me, so you won't have to make a real commitment. And you've succeeded, haven't you?' she finished bitterly.

'I certainly haven't suceeded in making you understand,' he said, and for the first time she could hear the anger in his voice. 'If I'm to be selective in my commitments, how long do you think our marriage will last? Until the first time I find myself feeling confined? I've never had to answer to anyone, and there will be times when I'll miss my independence. What am I supposed to do then about my commitment to you?'

'You don't need to worry,' she told him coldly. 'You've still got your independence, and you're obviously not about to give it up. It doesn't appear that I'm one of your precious commitments.' She turned away to stare blindly out the window.

'Well, you are,' he said wearily, 'but it's clear that you don't believe that.' He got to his feet and she could hear him moving as he dressed and gathered up his belongings. 'It's clear that you aren't going to believe me, and there's only one way to settle this. I'll leave you now. It's going to be three months—four at the most. But I am coming back to you.' He hesitated for an instant. 'I love you, and I need you, and I *am* coming back to you. I'll be back by the end of November, at the latest.' There was a long silence, while she knew he was watching her. 'There's nothing else to say, is there?' he finally asked, his voice empty as he turned to go.

After Simon left, nothing mattered except the pain and the emptiness and the occasional flashes of anger. Later, Victoria would look back on that time and realize that she had been incapable of thinking or acting rationally. There were days when she couldn't eat, and times when she was possessed by manic energy, walking for miles until exhaustion forced her back to the house. One particularly vivid memory was of the day she'd taken a pair of scissors and cut her long hair. Simon had said he loved it; now she would at least be spared that reminder of the way he had toyed with her!

Out of all her pain finally came the resolve that she

would never again beg for love. She had humiliated herself beyond belief during those times when she had pleaded with him to stay and make love to her. Never again would she debase herself to such an extent; never again would she allow anyone to matter that much to her! In the future, she would rely only on herself.

Simon had at least taught her that, although she hated him for the way in which he'd forced her to learn the lesson. She hated everything about him, even while his desertion left her with an aching void, wondering if she'd ever be able to escape from the nightmare world in which he'd left her.

Salvation came in the autumn, when her lonely summer ended and she began her job with *Global News*. She found a one-room apartment near the office in Concord and began to make a few friends. There was a comradeship among the small staff, a casual closeness which automatically included Victoria. They all recognised that the New Hampshire bureau was a less than choice assignment. New Hampshire didn't generate a great deal of news, but it was a place to start. Victoria was part of a young and agressive group, and their determination to move on created bonds of superficial friendship.

But none of the staff tried harder to move on than Victoria. She deliberately immersed herself in her job—working longer hours, searching out possible stories and reporting them to the very best of her ability. She found that to be the best way to forget, the only way to put Simon behind her. She thought of him occasionally and unwillingly, during the autumn and early winter. This was the time when he'd said he'd come back to her, and the fact that he didn't was confirmation that she'd been right.

By spring, her work had attracted enough attention to result in a transfer to the Boston bureau. This was a definite step up, and Victoria gladly accepted it. Boston offered more news, more opportunities to excel, and an infinitely more interesting place to live. She could lose herself in city life and find ever more superficial friendships to fill her time.

She even began to go out with men again, having refused all offers during her months in Concord. She had no intention of getting involved with anyone, but she saw no harm in an occasional evening out. So long, she reminded herself, as she kept it cool and casual and permitted no real closeness. If she dated a man who showed signs of becoming serious, she immediately broke things off. She saw no point in complications and she grew expert at avoiding them.

That wasn't hard to manage, because none of the men she met mattered at all to her. It wasn't that Simon had mattered so much that no one else could compare. What Simon had done was teach her that she must not let anyone matter. If you cared, you would be hurt—that was what she had learned from Simon Durant.

By the time a year had passed, she was well pleased with her life and able to view it with considerable satisfaction. She was doing well in her work and she had a promising future before her. What she didn't realise was that she had eliminated all emotion from her life. She had no awareness of the shell she had carefully constructed around herself. She would have hotly denied its existence, if anyone had tried to point it out to her. But no one did; no one knew her well enough to see the brittle shell, or the hurt beneath.

It was then, a year later, that Simon attempted to re-enter her life. Her first warning came when she returned to her desk, late one afternoon, to find among her messages one which simply gave his name and a local telephone number.

She stared at it for a few minutes before she crumpled

it up and threw it away. If she felt anything at all, it was merely faint surprise that he'd have the nerve to try to contact her again. Did he really expect her to welcome him with open arms? Did he think she was such a fool as to be willing to pick up where he evidently felt they'd left off? Was she supposed to love him again, allow herself to be hypnotised by him until he chose to leave her the next time? She was well over Simon Durant. He meant nothing to her, and she deliberately put the thought of him from her mind.

But he was not so easily dismissed when, two evenings later, she heard a knock at her apartment door and opened it to find him standing there. For a long moment, neither of them said anything. During that time, Victoria noted that he didn't seem to have changed at all. He still seemed a little too thin, a little too worn—the result, she supposed, of continuing to honour commitments more important than she had been.

'Hello, Victoria,' he finally said, and she was pleased to see that he was obviously ill at ease. That fact did wonders for her own sense of self-possession. 'It's taken me days to find you,' he continued after a brief hesitation. 'It took a while before anyone in Concord would tell me that you'd moved on to Boston. I only found out a couple of days ago. I left a message for you, but you may not have received it.' He paused and, when she made no response, she saw the brief flicker of uncertainty in his eyes. 'Could I come in, for just a few minutes at least?' he asked uneasily.

'I don't see any point to that,' she answered calmly. She felt enormously calm; in fact, she felt nothing at all, except a vague sense of satisfaction in knowing that he was uncertain and she was not.

'Victoria,' he tried again, 'I owe you an explanation and an apology.'

'No, Simon,' she said firmly. 'You're a year too late, and you don't owe me anything at all.'

'I want to explain—explain why it's been so long. I can, if you'll let me.'

'I don't need any explanation,' she said coolly. 'It may come as a surprise to you, but I'm really not interested.'

'Victoria, please!' She saw the mute appeal in his eyes and felt a marvellous sense of power because he was feeling something of what she'd felt when he'd left her. 'You don't mean that,' he said softly, with an almost pleading note.

'But I do.'

'Not after what we meant to each other.' He took a step towards her. 'You can't mean that. Please, Victoria. We loved each other. We still do,' he breathed, touching her face lightly.

For an instant, his touch frightened her, and then she remembered how she had clung to him once, how she had begged him to stay and to love her. Suddenly, she realised that he no longer had the power to move her or to make her care. That was gone, and in its place was her power to hurt him as much as he had hurt her.

She stepped back a pace so that she was free of his touch. 'Perhaps you still do,' she said without emotion, 'but I don't.' Then she suddenly realised exactly what she could do to hurt him even more. 'You've been gone too long, Simon,' she explained with cool self-possession. 'I've met someone else.' She hesitated for just an instant. 'We're going to be married in a couple of months. So you'll understand, I hope, if I'm not wildly excited at your sudden reappearance. It's very poor timing, and you're being almost too dramatic,' she finished with a pitying smile.

'I see,' he said carefully, his face rigid. 'I've obviously made a mistake.'

'Yes, you have,' she agreed evenly. 'We really haven't anything more to say to each other, have we?' She waited for just a moment, savouring the look of pain in his eyes, and then closed the door in his face.

As easy as that! she told herself with a feeling of triumph. She'd succeeded in hurting him as easily as that! He hadn't begged and pleaded as she had, but that wasn't his style. Besides, she hadn't given him the chance. For a moment, she almost wished she had, so that she could have enjoyed her victory even more. And it was a victory, she told herself. She felt an enormous sense of accomplishment. She had succeeded in hurting Simon, and in the process, she had accomplished something more. She had freed herself completely from her bondage to him. It was over now; it had ended.

It seemed marvellously appropriate when, two months later, *Global News* had offered her a transfer to the New York bureau. This was a definite promotion, the beginning of a new and glorious life. It was time for a new life, she told herself. She'd put Simon completely behind her and start her new life.

CHAPTER FIVE

Now, five years later, Victoria realised how wrong she'd been. It hadn't ended, and she hadn't put Simon behind her. The memories wouldn't be so fresh and clear, the feelings still so intense, if it had really ended. All night she'd turned restlessly in her bed, allowing herself to be again possessed by him. It was all so real—her initial fascination and their growing closeness, the feeling of belonging to him, and desire. She admitted that painfully, turning her head into the pillow. There had been that aching, uncontrollable need for him—something she'd never felt before, and something she'd never allowed herself to feel again.

Through the years, she had gone out with other men, but the relationships had been brief and casual and all of them had stopped well short of physical intimacy. She realised now that her feelings for Simon were what had caused her restraint. He'd become an unconscious standard against which she measured any man, and against which any man failed. But Simon had been more than a standard; he had also been an object lesson. Because of him, she'd refused to let any man matter to her. She'd refused to allow any man the power to move her and then hurt her, as Simon had.

She'd lived five empty years because of him. She'd been, in her own way, no better than he had been—seeking isolation, using it like a crutch. As the sky grew light, her thoughts became clearer and more composed. It was time to be free of Simon Durant; it was time to rid herself of him. And the only way to do that was to face the reality of him without flinching.

She had the means to do it; she was sure she did. An insane coincidence had given her what she needed. She could finally see him clearly, for what he really was. Even better, she could thread the pieces together and make sense of the random fragments. Best of all was the knowledge that she had the power to destroy his life, just as he had destroyed hers.

Although she hadn't really slept, she wasn't tired when she got up. She felt curiously calm and clear-headed, knowing exactly how she meant to proceed. Before she left for the office, she went to the bookshelves, knowing where to look as she pulled two books from their places and stuffed them into her battered briefcase. She'd need them for her research, once she reached the office.

The restrained confusion of the newsroom was comforting as she poured her first cup of coffee and retreated to her own desk. She had to start by working out a few rough facts on Simon. She needed dates and places to use, to anchor the name to some verifiable details.

And just what did she know? she asked herself, pulling a sheet of paper in front of her and beginning to sketch quick designs. She didn't even know how old Simon was. Still, he had once suggested that he was ten to fifteen years older than she. That would have made him thirty-two to thirty-seven when she'd known him. It was strange to think that she'd never before stopped to consider his age. He had obviously been older than she—older and vastly more experienced—but such details hadn't mattered to her at the time. Now it was vital that she know more, that she have as many firm facts as possible.

It was shocking to realize just how little he had revealed of himself. He'd said almost nothing until that last morning, and then he'd said so much so quickly that she hadn't been able to comprehend it all. But the firm facts she needed lay in what he had told her that morning. She had to force herself to remember his words and make some sense of them.

The sounds of the busy newsroom receded as she forced her thoughts back to that last morning. He'd left school and run away from his last foster home when he was fifteen. That much was easy to recall, and she deliberately closed her mind to what had happened immediately before and after his recital of the facts.

'I knocked around, finding work where I could,' he had told her. 'I made a bit of money at one thing and another—heavy construction, working in oil fields. Jobs like that aren't very pleasant, but they pay well. In my spare time, I made a point of staying out of other people's way. That's when I started reading anything I could get my hands on. After a few years of that, I decided I wanted an education—as wild an idea as it was.

'You see, I was poorly equiped to get an education,' he had continued dispassionately. 'I'd played truant for years, even before I'd dropped out of school. It took a bit of doing before I could even manage a high school diploma. But I did it with something of a flair—proving some obscure point to myself, I suppose. But it helped, and I found that there were a number of colleges interested in accepting me. I was,' he had explained self-consciously, 'a juvenile delinquent who'd managed to turn himself into an honour student—something of a novelty, the sort academic types use for experimentation. Brilliant but disadvantaged,' he had added with a mocking smile.

'So I went to college, with some scholarship help and the last of my oil field earnings, and found that I had a natural talent for languages. I seemed to pick them up without any trouble at all, which is what got me started on this whole business of war. The army is always looking for people like me—people who can easily catch on to odd languages and who know how to live by their wits. There aren't many of us and I was wonderfully well qualified, so there was an intensive effort to recruit me as soon as I'd graduated. Having never lived any normal sort of life, I wasn't going to object to the kind of insanity they were offering. I actually found the whole idea intriguing.

'So I enlisted, went through basic training and then Ranger Training. I was showing great promise at this sort of thing——' There had been, for an instant, a shading of distaste in his voice. 'I was showing so much promise that I was sent to Malaysia, to the British Jungle Tracking School. That's where you really learn the game. They're experts at it, and they make it very real. They send you out as part of a team, and then they capture you and give you a taste of what would happen if it weren't still a game. And then they keep sending you out until you've learned enough to avoid the end of the game. It *was* effective,' he had added with a complete absence of expression.

At the time, Victoria had wondered what he'd meant by that statement, exactly what he'd been forced to endure. Now, she didn't really care. What might have happened to Simon didn't matter to her. Facts were what mattered to her, and she needed more of them.

He'd told her about his time in the army, giving her details about his missions and mentioning that he'd been wounded on the last one. He'd gestured briefly towards the scar on his shoulder when he'd told her that. 'When I was on my feet again, they decided I'd done enough sacrificing,' he continued with a curious smile. 'I wasn't given any more missions. They made me an instructor, which I considered a far greater sacrifice. There was too much regimentation, too little independence. I found that it didn't suit me, so I got out as soon as possible.

'But then I was lost,' he had explained. 'I did a little writing, but that wasn't what I wanted. I'd enjoyed my missions—in a peculiar sort of way. I liked depending on myself and trusting nothing but my instincts. That sort of life strips away all the non-essentials. There's nothing civilised about living that close to the edge. You're down to absolute basics, with nothing to think about except surviving and getting the job done.

'And God, how I loved it,' he had continued with a frightening intensity. 'I didn't like the killing, but that was the price I had to pay. None of it would have meant a thing, without the constant threat of death. Still, I could have done without the killing—I still could, for that matter. But it's all I know, and I've become extraordinarily adept at finding opportunities for guerrilla warfare, at making contacts and offering my services.'

Abruptly, Victoria pulled her thoughts back to the present. She didn't want to go on to what had happened next, when she had found herself begging him to stay. She'd relived that particular humiliation last night; there was no need to go through it again.

Hurriedly, she began to make notes, particularly trying to work out the dates of Simon's army service. There wasn't much to go on, she thought glumly, and most of that was guess work. Still, unless he'd lied to her, there were some facts which could be checked by the research department. Victoria brought her notes down to Ginny Howe, who occasionally did the impossible in turning up information.

'Do you suppose you could find me anything about this man?' Victoria asked Ginny, handing over her notes. 'I'll take anything at all.'

Ginny scanned the paper quickly. 'I can get a birth

certificate—unofficially, of course. I'm not sure about the rest of it, except for his army record. That's probably the best bet.'

'The army record is what I'm most interested in, anyway,' Victoria explained. 'That's where I really need to start.'

Ginny nodded. 'I'll find you something.' She glanced back at the sheet of paper. 'An interesting story here,' she said thoughtfully and then looked up at Victoria. 'Tell me something. Is he a hero or a villain?'

'That all depends,' Victoria answered casually, turning away from Ginny's desk.

'Depends on what?' Ginny called after her.

'The person you ask, I suppose.' Some people would consider Simon a hero, she reflected as she made her way back to her desk. People who hadn't known him as she had, she thought bitterly. If she were right about the next step in her research, she was about to learn that a lot of people did consider him a marvellous kind of hero, but those would be people who didn't know him at all.

Next, she settled at her desk with another cup of coffee and opened her briefcase. Now came the moment of truth, she thought uneasily. The two books she was about to look at wouldn't prove anything by themselves. But possibly, coupled with what Ginny might find for her, she'd have confirmation of her theory. If she did, then Simon would learn how it felt to have his world shattered, just as she had when he'd shattered hers.

She pulled the two books from her briefcase and set them on her desk, clearing a space for them. Both had been authored by Peter Soule, although the publisher had made it very clear that the name was merely a pseudonym. The first book, *Under Starlight*, had been a very personal account of one young man's experiences as a member of an army Special Forces team. The book had created an instant sensation, receiving critical praise while remaining for weeks on the best-seller lists. There had been enormous speculation about the true identity of the author—endless analyses in the press and hypothetical profiles. But no name had ever emerged. The publisher had resolutely refused to provide any information, and the author had never given himself away. In spite of the public's fascination with a young man's ability to combine action with deep insight and introspection, he had never been identified.

In time, the sensation had passed, only to start again when his second book had come out, three years ago. This one, *A Sure Defeat*, had dealt with the author's experiences after his discharge from the army, with his involvement in guerrilla warfare in remote parts of the world. The second book had been even more enthusiastically received, and Victoria took a moment to read the critics' quotes printed on the dust jacket: '... faces the realities—and insanities—of war with depth and maturity,' said one, while another hailed it as '... powerful and beautifully written; a damning indictment of war.'

They were great reviews, Victoria reflected. The book had been another best seller, creating an even greater demand by the public to learn the identity of Peter Soule. But there had been absolutely no break, not even a rumour. No one knew who Peter Soule really was, except his publisher. And, Victoria told herself with a sudden feeling of confidence, herself.

She started with *Under Starlight*, which had come out during her second year in college. Like everyone else she knew, she had read it. She'd read it several times, in fact, captivated by the author's perception and sensitivity and his understanding of loneliness and isolation. Those were qualities she'd understood and shared. Much of what he'd said had spoken directly to her; she, too, knew what it was to live without ties and attachments.

She hesitated for a moment and then opened the book to read the first lines:

'I watch the stars. Stars are grand companions.
Their lonely existence is something I can understand.
Detachment and a safe distance from the world have served them well—and must serve me.'

'I watch the stars,' she repeated to herself, allowing her thoughts to drift back to the first night, when he'd brought her home from Mira's party.

'Stars are another of my weaknesses,' he'd said, leaning against the side of the house while she hunted for her key. 'I watch the stars. They're grand companions.'

It couldn't be coincidence, she told herself as she stared with almost morbid fascination at the words. The only thing she didn't understand was why she hadn't made the connection long ago. She ought to have, even at the time he'd said the words. But she hadn't been analysing things then; she'd been too caught up in the novelty and the wonder of the man.

Still, it was hard to believe that she'd never consciously made the connection. The author's name should have given her clues. The day after the party, she'd asked Simon his middle name and he'd told her that he had only the one he'd created for himself: Peter. The night they'd met, he'd said he was a solitary soul. There had been amusement in his voice, as though the two of them had been sharing a private joke. They had; it was only that she hadn't understood it at the time. It seemed that he'd almost deliberately been testing her, trying to see if she would realise who he was.

Now, it all seemed highly suggestive, almost

conclusive, but she needed facts which could be verified. Her task now was to go through the books and note specific details to check against whatever she could learn about Simon Durant. She couldn't go to Tim without hard facts.

By late afternoon, when Ginny arrived at her desk, Victoria had made great progress and her note pad was filling up. When she saw Ginny, she straightened up, wearily rubbing the small of her back. 'Anything at all?' she asked hopefully.

'Some.' Ginny nodded, pulling over a chair and consulting her notes as she sat down. 'Not as much as you might like,' she added doubtfully.

'I'll take anything, right now.'

'Well, it's pretty sketchy. There's only his military record—such as it is. It's got holes in it, because a lot of it is obviously classified.'

'Let me hear it,' Victoria said, sipping her cold coffee before picking up her pen.

'He volunteered, was commissioned a Second Lieutenant in July, 1972. Then it's pretty much what you told me—basic training, advanced basic, jump school, followed by time at the Royal British Jungle Tracking School. Then he was assigned to a Special Mission Team, second in command. There's nothing about what the team did—that's obviously classified.

'Rapid advancement,' Ginny continued. 'By 1974, he'd made Captain and was commanding his own team. He was wounded, late that year—in the shoulder, if that's any help.' She looked up quickly while Victoria tried to keep her face carefully expressionless, remembering the scar she'd discovered on Simon's shoulder. 'He was hospitalised for the wound and for treatment of malaria. After that, he was an instructor in advanced basic training until he requested discharge in the summer of 1975.

'Here's a list of the places he was, when he wasn't in the other places they've carefully left out—classified again.' She laid the list on Victoria's desk and then returned to her other notes. 'Much decorated, although you don't get the usual explanations of what he did to get the decorations. I expect that's classified, too. He's got a Distinguished Service Cross, Bronze and Silver Stars, a Purple Heart—not too bad. I think you'd have to say he's a hero,' she finished thoughtfully, obviously remembering the question she'd asked earlier.

'That's open to debate,' Victoria observed dryly and caught Ginny's questioning look. 'It's not my business to decide which,' she explained. 'All I'm going to do is be objective about a story.'

'*Is* he a story?' Ginny asked. 'I've never heard of him.'

'That's the point,' Victoria said with a smile. 'No one has, but I think everyone is about to,' she added with a quick feeling of triumph.

The next morning, Victoria presented herself at Simon's publishing house. She'd spent the evening checking Ginny's list of places mentioned in his military record against the places in the book. In every case, they matched perfectly. It was hard to understand why no one had ever seen the parallels before, but she supposed it was simply that no one had ever known which man's military record to check.

When she explained her purpose to the receptionist, she was allowed to see an associate editor who greeted her with considerable reserve.

'You have to understand, Miss Ward,' he explained carefully, 'we never have, and never will, discuss the identity of Peter Soule.'

'It's *Ms* Ward,' Victoria said sweetly, resenting his condescension. 'And I haven't come to ask *you* to discuss the identity of Peter Soule. *I've* come to discuss it, and to give you a chance to comment, if you like.'

'A number of reporters have already done that, and it's never done any good.' He smiled blandly.

'But none of them knew he was Simon Durant, did they?' she asked casually, and then waited for a reaction.

There wasn't one. He merely smiled again. 'You understand that I'll neither confirm nor deny that statement,' he said easily. 'Some reporters can make as much of a denial as a confirmation, so we make it a practice to do neither.'

'But I'm not that kind of reporter,' Victoria explained with a smile of her own. 'I don't intend to do anything with a denial. I intend to go with a story I know is true.'

'Backed up with any facts?' he asked with a hint of sarcasm.

'A great many.'

'Others have tried that, too.' He sounded almost regretful.

'The others weren't right. I am.'

'Others have said that, too.' He rose, leaving Victoria in no doubt that the interview was over.

'If you decide that you'd like to discuss this further, you can reach me here.' She laid her card on his desk. 'There's still time. I don't intend to release the story until Mr Durant has returned from Afghanistan.' With a feeling of triumph—the second in as many days—she saw the brief flicker of concern before he carefully composed his face.

'I'm afraid you won't be hearing from me,' he answered smoothly, escorting her to the door.

'Then you—and Mr Durant—will be hearing from me, won't you?' she asked pleasantly as she left the room.

* * *

By late afternoon, her notes were in order. Every possible fact had been neatly linked to others and Victoria was confident of her story. When she went into Tim's office, she had all her arguments ready.

'Would we like to be the ones to break the story of who Peter Soule really is?' she asked without preliminaries. 'Exactly who he is—names and dates and places, and no room for debate?'

'Anyone would like to break that story.' Tim whistled. 'Is that what you've got?'

'That's exactly what I've got.'

He swore softly under his breath. 'It sounds just a little improbable, you know. You're telling me that a man walked out on you, five years ago, and now you've discovered that he's Peter Soule.'

'That's right,' she agreed, ignoring his scepticism.

'Are you sure that you've been entirely logical about this? That you haven't just blown something out of proportion, because of an unhappy experience with a man you obviously haven't been able to forget?'

'I'm very sure!' she snapped. 'And you would be, too, if you'd stop psychoanalysing me and listen to what I have to say.'

He nodded, looking less than convinced. 'Show me what you have.'

So Victoria started, working steadily through her notes, backing each statement with references to Simon's book, or to his military record. It made a convincing presentation, and she knew it. She'd filled in as many of the gaps as possible and found every conceivable link between the two names. 'It's there,' she finished with conviction. 'He couldn't deny it, and he couldn't sue.'

'He could deny it,' Tim pointed out reasonably, 'but he couldn't sue. He wouldn't, anyway. He wouldn't want the publicity. And you're right—it's all there.'

'Then I'm not just a neurotic woman who's been scorned?' she asked, amused.

'Oh, well—you may be that, too.' Tim grinned. 'But I accept your facts and I could go with them, except for one thing.'

'What thing?' she demanded, wondering what she could possibly have missed.

'The story doesn't go far enough. It stops almost ten years ago. If we go with what you've got, we leave half the story for someone else to tell. What has Peter Soule been doing the rest of the time? You've only given me the first half of the story.'

'The rest won't be as easy to check,' she explained reasonably. 'He left military service, so there won't be any records. There is his second book which gives details of guerrilla fighting, but they can't be checked—not without a awful lot of digging.'

'There's one other way. I'm surprised you didn't think of it.' He leaned back in his chair and eyed her curiously. 'An interview, Vicky,' he prompted, when she said nothing. 'Maybe a whole series of them. All you've got to do is interview him,' Tim finished cheerfully.

'You're mad! He'd never permit it.'

'He wouldn't?' Tim asked carefully. 'Or is it that you couldn't?'

'Of course I could!' she snapped. 'I could, if he'd let me. But he's not going to let anyone interview him—least of all me.'

'You most of all, I should have thought. You wouldn't be coming at him as a reporter. You'd be *his* Ghost of Christmas Past—that sweet young thing he loved and left, five years ago. You could get to him where no one else could.'

'I don't think you quite realise how things ended between us,' Victoria said warily. 'It's not as though we parted friends.'

'But that was five years ago.' Tim brushed her objection aside. 'Who knows how he feels about you now? And does it really matter? I'm betting he'd see you—out of curiosity, if nothing else. And, once he'd seen you, I'm betting you could get the interview. No one else is going to get one—that's the safest bet of all.'

'I don't think it would work.' She shifted uneasily. 'I never gave it a thought.'

'I know you didn't give it a thought,' Tim agreed mildly. 'But you ought to, unless it would make you too uncomfortable. Are you sure there aren't just a few raw nerves left?'

'Very sure,' she answered steadily. For the last two days, she'd thought about nothing but Simon Durant and the wonder of it was that she'd finally succeeded in laying the ghost. At some point during that time, he'd stopped being Simon, the knight-errant who had continued to exist beneath the pain and bitterness. He'd become Simon Durant, an abstraction, a story. 'There wouldn't be any problem,' she said firmly.

'Then start thinking about an interview,' Tim said briskly. 'All we have to do is wait until he gets back here, and then go to it.'

'While I'm waiting, could you get the stringer in Peshawar to find out what he can?' Victoria asked quickly. 'That's part of the story, after all.'

'Oh, I've already done that,' Tim said blandly. 'Haven't heard anything yet, but I've got the word to him and he'll be picking up anything he can.'

'Then you *did* think I had something!'

'No, I really didn't,' Tim said calmly, ignoring her enthusiasm. 'But I figured there was nothing to lose. We're paying him to listen to rumours, so there was no reason why he shouldn't listen to a few more.'

'Will you let me know, as soon as you get anything?' she asked eagerly.

'Of course I will. And in the meantime, I'd keep my mouth shut, if I were you. Your good friend, Ken, has been nosing around, wanting to know what your angle is. Now go back to work,' he finished kindly, 'and keep your notes locked up, too.'

It was an anticlimax, for the next two weeks, to work on routine stories. Victoria knew she was on to something big, and it was difficult to concentrate on things that didn't seem to matter. It was, she realised, a matter of being patient, of waiting until Simon came out of Afghanistan and returned to this country. Then there would be the task of finding him and getting to see him. Only then would she have her story. And her revenge, she admitted only rarely. Most of the time, she didn't bother to think about that aspect of the matter. Simon continued to be an abstraction—not the man she had once loved and now despised.

During the two weeks, Tim had little to report. The stringer in Peshawar had passed on very little—only a few rumours about Simon's movements in Afghanistan during the summer. At the moment, it seemed that no one was quite sure where he was.

'How do we know he hasn't left the country?' Victoria asked nervously, after Tim had shared the latest report with her.

'It's very simple, as a matter of fact,' Tim assured her. 'One thing our fellow has found out is that a room, and a few of his things, are being held for him in one of the hotels in Peshawar. And a few of the leaders who make that area their base of operations have said that the American is going to come back to talk to them, before he leaves. So he'll come out through Peshawar, and we'll hear when he does.'

Still, in spite of her impatience, Victoria hadn't expected

to hear quite so soon, and she certainly hadn't expected to hear what she did. It was only a few days later, only three weeks since the whole business had started, that Tim called her into his office.

'We may have a slight change in plans,' he began without delay. 'I think your man is on his way out. This just came in over the wire, and it's the most definite word yet.' He rapidly scanned the information on the paper. 'A rebel who was wounded in the fighting two weeks ago made it back to the Red Cross Hospital in Peshawar. His unit had been fighting in the same area as the one Durant is leading. According to our stringer, this fellow had seen Durant several times. He said that the American had broken his leg and was about to head back to Peshawar. It seems likely that he'll get himself back and installed in the hospital, at least for a while.'

'And how long until he gets back here?' Victoria asked moodily, wondering if her story would ever see the light of day.

'I don't see that it matters,' Tim said cheerfully. '*You're* going to go to Peshawar and meet him there.'

'I'm *what*?' she demanded.

'You heard me.' He grinned. 'It makes perfect sense. It will give the story considerably more interest, and you'll have a better understanding of the background. It also seems likely that it will give you a certain psychological edge in getting an interview. You'll be a familiar face—probably the only one. And, if he's in a hospital with a broken leg, he won't have much opportunity to take evasive action, will he?'

'I don't suppose,' Victoria said doubtfully, trying to think this all through. 'It almost seems like taking unfair advantage of him,' she finished uneasily.

'Well, if you don't want to be unfair——' Tim let the words hang in the air.

'I never said that,' she contradicted swiftly. In fact,

the thought of being unfair suddenly seemed a marvellous idea. There was a certain poetic justice in being unfair to Simon Durant—just as he'd once been so unfair to her. 'When do I leave?' she asked firmly.

Tim smiled, as though he'd just won a bet with himself. 'It depends on how up to date you are on your cholera shots, I suppose,' he answered casually.

'I've never had one in my life.'

'Then you can start this afternoon, and you'll need another a week from today. Here's the name and address of the doctor who will give them to you, and a list of the other things you'll have to have.'

'Not for a week?' she demanded.

'It's not as bad as it sounds,' he consoled her. 'It beats getting cholera or malaria. And the rebel did say that Durant wasn't planning to start back immediately. The two of you might arrive in Peshawar at just about the same time.

'And by the way,' he continued more seriously, 'for the record, Global is sending you to Peshawar to do a series on the refugee problem there. That way, your real story doesn't become known.' He smiled and then got to his feet.

'Are you *sure* that I'm not going to miss him, if I wait a week?' Victoria asked uneasily. Now that she knew she was going, she wanted to be on her way immediately.

'We couldn't do anything about it, even if you were.' Tim shrugged. 'But look on the bright side of things. It's going to be considerably more difficult for Durant to get across the border into Pakistan than it will be for you. And he's the one with the broken leg. That ought to slow him down,' he added with a grin.

Nothing slowed Victoria down, and exactly eight days later she found herself on an evening flight to Paris, the first stage of what promised to be a long journey. She'd been properly protected against cholera, malaria, polio, tetanus and typhoid, had her itinerary worked out and knew that she'd be met—when she finally did get to Peshawar—by the Global stringer.

The trip seemed endless; overnight to Paris and then a four-hour layover before her flight to Karachi. In Karachi, she was forced to wait eight hours for her connecting flight to Islamabad, managing to nap only fitfully in the waiting area. At the airport in Islamabad, she hired a car for the last leg of the trip. When she and her minimal luggage were finally installed in a battered Toyota, she had the consolation of knowing that a hotel room—and a bed—waited at the end of the journey.

As tired and hot and dirty as she felt, this last part of the trip was fascinating and kept her occupied. The congestion of Islamabad was left behind, and the mountains were visible in the distance as they crossed the Indus River. As they grew closer to Peshawar, Victoria studied the contrast between the lush, fertile lowland through which the car was travelling and the rocky peaks which almost completely surrounded the area.

Her driver spoke no English, so she couldn't question him. But she knew they were in the Vale of Peshawar, moving directly towards the heart of the former North-West Frontier Province which had been created in the nineteenth century by the British as a buffer zone against the warring Afghan tribes. Beyond Peshawar, she knew, lay the Khyber Pass where for centuries caravans had come down from Afghanistan to trade in the city's many markets.

This was history, she thought with a sudden surge of excitement, history and foreign travel with a vengeance. Join *Global News* and see the world, even though she was seeing almost too much of it at one gulp!

Peshawar, when they finally reached it, was a dusty world of confusion—the streets clogged with cars and trucks, horsedrawn carts, pack animals and motorised rickshaws, and more people than Victoria had ever before seen in the streets of a city. The congestion made New York's rush hour look like marvellous organisation, and it seemed to take hours for the car to inch through the mass of humanity and the dust.

But the hotel was reassuring, a low structure with white-washed walls and a comparative air of serenity about it. Inside the long, narrow lobby it was cooler and quiet except for the steady creaking of the overhead fans which provided some circulation of air.

The stringer—bless his heart, Victoria thought gratefully—was waiting for her. Rahim Khan was a slight, dark-complexioned young man with a willing air and a cheerful smile. Best of all, he spoke perfect English with only the slightest of accents. He handled her registration with a minimum of effort, speaking whatever language it was that people spoke in Peshawar—Victoria couldn't remember because she was so tired—and then hesitantly suggested that she join him in the hotel's dining room for something to eat.

'You must want to sleep,' he explained, 'but you would sleep better, if you ate first.'

It made perfect sense to Victoria, perhaps because she was past the point of trying to analyse anything. According to her watch, it was seven in the morning, but it was late afternoon at the hotel. She reckoned that she'd now been up for over forty-eight hours, and the feeling was quite unlike anything she had ever before experienced.

She followed Rahim into the dining room and gratefully sipped several cups of strong black tea while she made an effort to eat something—she was never sure just what it was. The tea helped to wash some of the dust from her throat and was sufficiently bracing to give her a semblance of coherence, enough to ask Rahim if there had been any further word on Simon Durant.

'Only today, from a wounded mujahideen who came into the hospital. He told me he left Asnar almost two weeks ago, but that he heard, before he left, that the American had already started out. That area is about a hundred miles north of here.'

'Then why isn't Durant here by now?' Victoria asked, surprised that she could muster such a logical question.

Rahim shrugged. 'He said the American had been at Wama, a little further into the mountains. It could take longer for him to get out. But he will come here,' he continued with a pleased smile. 'Precisely here, unless he goes first to the hospital. You see, this is the hotel where he arranged to leave his things and have a room held. I did very well,' he added with poorly concealed pride, 'to see that you also stayed here.'

'Very well,' Victoria agreed almost absently. 'But I still don't see why it would take him longer. If he had already started out, before the man you talked to today...' She trailed off uncertainly.

'But you must understand that much depends on the route,' Rahim explained earnestly. 'Some are more difficult than others, and there is always the chance that the Russians will make it more difficult still. Sometimes there are bombing raids, and other times they drop the butterfly mines. It is better, you understand, at times like that, to wait or to go very slowly.'

Victoria wasn't at all sure she understood, particularly about the butterfly mines which meant nothing to her. But that could wait until morning, she decided abruptly, realising that she wasn't capable of any more conversation until she'd had some sleep.

Within a very few minutes, she'd been led through a labyrinth of corridors to her small room. There was a shower room just down the hall, and sufficient tepid water to wash away the accumulated grime of her trip. Her room was dim and filled with shadows, and she could hear nothing but the monotonous stirring of the ceiling fan as she crawled into bed. She ached all over, and the thought suddenly occured to her that life as a foreign correspondent wasn't nearly as glamorous as some people thought. It was, in fact, tiring and surprisingly disorientating.

Unbidden, she found herself remembering the night Simon had come back to her. He'd said that he was fighting jet lag and culture shock, and Victoria suddenly knew exactly how he felt. But it was better not to think about Simon, at least not in relation to that particular time. She could think about him as an abstract concept—as a story—but that was all. She would not think about him as the man he had once been to her. For a moment, that thought was firmly fixed in her mind, and then she was instantly asleep.

CHAPTER SIX

VICTORIA came awake the next morning at dawn, startled by a high, piercing cry unlike anything she'd ever heard before. She lay without moving for a moment, trying to identify the sound, trying to work out where she was, for that matter. Then it came to her: she was hearing the muezzin, calling the faithful to prayer. She had read about that, only a few days before.

'Do not sleep,' the book had explained the muezzin's call. 'Prayer is better than sleep.'

She was in Pakistan, she remembered. In Peshawar, to be precise. At the moment, she and the muezzin didn't see eye to eye. Sleep was better than anything, even prayer. So she turned on her side and went immediately back to sleep.

The next time she woke, her room was almost uncomfortably warm and bright with light reflected off the white-washed wall beyond her window. She glanced automatically at her watch and then realised that it could tell her nothing at all. Her watch was still set to New York time, and she was somewhere else entirely. She was also hungry, she discovered, feeling surprisingly human now. She'd obviously slept long enough—however long that had been—and she was ready to face the day.

After another shower, with slightly warmer water this time, she dressed quickly in a pair of jeans and a thin cotton shirt. Then she worked her way back through the labyrinth of corridors until she found the lobby. The desk clerk (in Peshawar, did one call him a desk clerk? she wondered) clearly recognised her and hurried to give her a slip of paper.

It was a note from Rahim, carefully printed and to the point. 'I will come back at two, or at six, if you are still sleeping.' That was no help at all, she realised, glancing at her useless watch.

'Could you tell me the time?' she asked the clerk, but he obviously didn't understand. 'The time,' she repeated stupidly and then pointed to her watch and fixed him with an enquiring look.

Obligingly, he nodded and produced his own watch to show her the time. His said one o'clock and she set hers to the same, mentally saying good bye to New York.

If Rahim was planning to come at two, she had time to eat, so she went into the dining room and managed to get a meal by pointing to what others were having. She chose fruit and bread and cheese, trusting that her shots and pills would protect her from anything, and washed it all down with more of the strong black tea. By the time Rahim appeared, she felt ready for anything.

For the next three days, Victoria found herself becoming increasingly frustrated. She and Rahim spent long hours haunting the Red Cross Hospital, checking with all his sources among the refugee and rebel leadership, and even driving out to visit the nearest refugee camps outside the city.

Rahim had to make all the enquiries, of course, since no one spoke English. The conversations were in Pushtu, always beginning with the greeting, 'Asalamalaikum'—'peace be with you'. It seemed a strange thing to say, when the subject was always war and they were usually speaking with warriors, many of them having been wounded. Still, it was a part of this strange world, like the five times a day when the muezzin called the faithful to prayer, or the tall Pathan tribesmen with their fierce black moustaches, loose trousers and blue or white turbans.

Victoria found herself treated with a scrupulous courtesy which bordered on a studied refusal to acknowledge her presence. She supposed that she wasn't a Pathan tribesman's idea of a proper woman. She was certainly quite unlike their own women, who were self-effacing in the extreme. They wore long, enveloping gowns and shawls which covered their heads and shoulders, in marked contrast to Victoria's habitual jeans and shirts and the sun hat she'd found in one of the street bazaars.

The days and the people blurred together, an endless succession of questions and answers during which she had to wait patiently for Rahim's translation. The translation was always the same. *If* 'the American' had been seen—and he hadn't been seen by many—he hadn't been seen in a while. He had always been somewhere—near Bagram, or Baricot, or Wama, or vaguely 'in the mountains'. It seemed to be an accepted fact among those who had seen him most recently, that he *was* coming out. But no one knew that he had, and no one could say when, or where, he would. It was, one dead end after another, until Victoria wanted to scream in frustration.

'It will take time,' Rahim observed helpfully as he brought her back to the hotel at the end of yet another futile day. 'The Russians are very active now, on the other side of the border. One proceeds with caution, you understand.'

'Other people are getting through,' Victoria pointed out.

'But others may have been lucky enough to choose easier routes, or may not have stopped along the way.

Mr Durant may have stopped to meet with others of the mujahideen. We will hear something soon,' he added cheerfully as he pulled up at the front of the hotel.

'We'd better,' Victoria said gloomily, as she got out of the battered little car and they agreed on a time to meet the next morning.

She found the shower room occupied, so she went back to her room and stretched out on the bed to wait until it was free. Predictably, she fell asleep and didn't wake up until well after dark. Furious with herself for having undoubtedly destroyed her night's sleep, she took her shower and then went along to the dining room for what she supposed would pass for fashionably late, in Peshawar.

It appeared that it wasn't fashionable to dine late in Peshawar; the dining room was nearly deserted. But Victoria's waiter seemed in no hurry, so she lingered after she had finished eating to drink more cups of tea and work on her scrambled notes from the day's searching. At the far end of the room, a group of Pakistani businessmen were taking even more time over their dinner than she had, occupying most of her waiter's time. Since she obviously wasn't delaying him, she stayed at her table. The light was better here than in her room and it was cooler, so she kept adding to her notes.

She had, by this time, a respectable amount of background information on the war, the rebel fighters, and the Afghan refugee problem. While she hadn't yet managed to find Simon Durant, she was acquiring a lot of useful details about the sort of war he had been fighting. When she finally did make contact with him and get her interview—*if* she made contact and got her interview, she amended quickly—she would have all she needed to end her story as Tim wanted it ended.

The days of waiting weren't going to be a complete waste, she told herself firmly. The more she learned, the more she would be able to get out of an interview with Simon. It was better to be positive about this whole business. Sooner or later, the days of waiting would pay off; Rahim was convinced of it, and she should be, too.

Reluctantly, she closed her notebook and prepared to leave the dining room. It was now well after midnight, the group of businessmen were obviously nearly done, and she couldn't spend the night in the dining room. She'd have to go back to her room and try to sleep, even though the combination of her nap and the tea had left her wide awake.

Nodding her thanks to the waiter, she started for the dining-room door. Just as she reached it, she turned, hearing the beginnings of a slight commotion at the street entrance to the lobby. Three men had just come into the building—tall, shadowy figures in the gloom. Two of them were talking loudly, in Pushtu, Victoria thought, and they looked to be Pathan tribesmen. All three were wearing the typical loose trousers and long shirts, but only the two who were talking had the turbans and fierce moustaches which were so characteristic of the Pathans. The third was bareheaded and clean shaven. Then she literally froze as the three men passed under one of the dim lights hanging from the ceiling.

It *can't* be, she told herself, resisting an hysterical urge to laugh or faint. She wasn't sure which would be most appropriate. It was entirely too improbable. Things simply didn't happen this way, and yet it seemed that they had. There was no mistaking the features of the third man. It was Simon, and she instantly accepted the inevitability of that fact.

The two tribesmen with him were doing all the talking, appearing to be arguing strenuously, while

Simon ignored them completely. He was walking stiffly, with an almost halting gait, his features rigid as he stared straight ahead. As Victoria watched, he reached the desk and gripped its edge, bracing himself against it. She saw him impatiently shake his head and speak briefly to the men on either side of him before turning to talk to the clerk who was now on his feet and instantly attentive.

And what was she going to do, she asked herself, trying to organise her thoughts. She supposed she could just stand here and watch; that might be best. But she was already moving slowly across the lobby, drawn by instinct. She reached the desk just as Simon turned away from it, and they were suddenly face to face, not five feet separating them.

Closer to him and in slightly better light, she could see how utterly ravaged he looked. Each line and angle of his face was emphasised, the skin stretched tautly over the bones beneath. He looked a little grey beneath his tan, and there were hectic traces of colour against his cheeks. For an instant he stared blankly at her, as though not seeing her at all.

Then his eyes seemed to focus and he frowned, looking slightly displeased. 'Why on earth have you cut your hair?' he asked curiously, as though he'd last seen her a week before. 'I don't like it,' he added absently and then turned back to the two tribesmen who were staring at her with disapproval. Simon spoke briefly to them in what sounded like Pushtu, gestured them away with considerable emphasis, and then nodded as he reached for her shoulder.

'You're going to have to help me out for a bit,' he began, his hand gripping her shoulder tightly. 'I know where my room is, and if you'll just walk that far with me, they'll be satisfied. It's a marvellous stroke of luck to have found you here. You're just what I need.' He was already moving, directing them both towards one of the corridors leading from the lobby.

Victoria was vaguely aware of the two Pathan tribesmen now regarding her with curiosity, and wondered exactly what Simon had said to them. But there wasn't much time to think of that, because he was continuing steadily on, his hand on her shoulder forcing her to keep pace with him.

They followed the various twists and turns, passing Victoria's own room in the process, and finally Simon halted the two of them before a closed door.

'Could you possibly manage the key for me?' he asked, passing it to her with his free hand, still gripping her shoulder with the other. As soon as she had opened the door and switched on the dim light, he released her.

'I think I'd better sit down,' he said carefully and then swore softly under his breath as he lowered himself on to the edge of the bed. He sat without moving for a moment and then nodded approvingly. 'That's better.' He shifted his left leg carefully, allowing it to straighten at an odd angle. 'Someone's going to bring along tea in a few minutes. You might get the door, when it comes. And there's a flight bag in the corner—over there.' He gestured briefly. 'If you'll hand it to me, you'll save me the effort.'

She passed it to him and then turned to open the door as she heard the discreet tap. It was the porter who silently offered the tea tray and then retreated. 'Shall I pour you a cup?' she asked, setting the tray down on the bureau.

'If you would,' he answered absently, searching through the flight bag, producing a couple of small medicine containers.

She poured a cup and handed it to him, his hand brushing hers briefly as he took the cup. 'I think you've got a temperature,' she said, realising just how hot his hand had felt against hers.

'Probably,' he agreed mildly. 'I've got any number of things, this time.' He bent his head to sip experimentally at the tea. 'I made two mistakes, you see,' he continued after a moment. 'The first was when I broke my leg. I jumped when I ought to have gone more slowly. That's an amateur's mistake, and inexcusable.'

'You can't possibly know that you've broken your leg,' Victoria objected.

'You can when you hear it happen,' he explained dispassionately. 'A thoroughly audible snap doesn't leave much room in your mind for doubt.' He drank some more tea and then set down the cup long enough to open the containers and take a couple of pills from each. He washed them down with the rest of the tea and then held out the cup for a refill. 'But we splinted it up quite effectively,' he resumed, as though discussing something as commonplace as a minor sprain. 'It didn't seem to cause any great problem, so I just kept going. Besides, I didn't see any reason to leave, just because I'd made a stupid mistake.'

'As good a reason as any to walk about a war zone on a broken leg,' Victoria observed dryly.

'Oh, it isn't quite a war zone anymore. The summer offensive is nearly over, so things are reasonably quiet—even dull on occasion.' He seemed to be gathering momentum as he talked, looking no better but sounding quite like himself. 'It was getting out that presented the biggest problem. It's not precisely dull near the border. The Russians are seeding the mountain passes with those damned butterfly mines. They're little bits of plastic, not half the size of my hand,' he explained, 'the colour of dirt and leaves. Pressure sets them off, and I was stupid enough not to look where I was walking. That was the second mistake. A good thing it happened to the same leg,' he added thoughtfully, more to himself than to her.

The whole thing was mad, she thought, letting herself down on to the straight chair by the bureau. He was behaving as though nothing at all had happened between them, as though the past five years had never existed. Even more insane was the fact that she was doing the same, listening to him as though he'd never left her. At the moment, she wasn't at all sure what she could do about the situation, or even if she wanted to do anything about it.

'Fortunately,' he continued after a moment, 'the one I stepped on was mostly under a rock. Not much of the shrapnel got to my leg. It did slow me down and it made it a bit more difficult to get out, but it could have been worse. It's really just a minor inconvenience, but my two friends there wanted to make something major out of it.' He pulled himself on to the bed, again carefully arranging his leg before he propped the pillow against the headboard and then leaned back against it. 'They thought I ought to go to the hospital here, but I'm not fond of hospitals. They think hospitals are marvellous places—they've never had one before. Now that the Red Cross has obligingly provided them with one, it's gone to their heads.' He stopped and rubbed his hand wearily over his eyes. 'I think something's gone to mine, too,' he said slowly. 'Nothing is making any sense at all.'

'That doesn't surprise me,' Victoria said without expression.

'No, I don't suppose it does,' he agreed absently and then looked up at her as though really seeing her for the first time. 'But what are you doing here?' he asked in confusion.

'I was waiting for you.'

'I don't see how.' He shifted restlessly. 'I didn't tell

you where I was going. Or did I? I really can't remember,' he trailed off vaguely and closed his eyes.

Victoria sat without moving, wondering what she ought to do. He looked sick, he was hurt, and whatever reserves of strength had been carrying him were obviously slipping away. It seemed that she ought to be doing something, but she couldn't think of a blessed thing. What he ought to have done was to have gone to the hospital, but he hadn't, and getting him there was clearly beyond her capabilities.

'It's getting confused,' he remarked idly, opening his eyes and looking blankly around the room. 'Not making any sense at all.' He suddenly began to shake uncontrollably, drawing his arms against his chest until the bout had passed. 'That's malaria,' he explained with clinical detachment. 'It's been coming on for a couple of days.'

'What should I do?' she asked briskly, getting to her feet.

'Oh, you don't *do* anything about malaria,' he said casually. 'It does as it pleases. But I'm cold,' he complained and began to shake again.

It was obvious that there was no way she was going to be able to move him enough to get him properly into bed, but she covered him with the one extra blanket and then eyed him doubtfully. He was still shivering and the blanket was clearly inadequate. But there were two more, she remembered, in her room somewhere down the hall.

She told him she'd be right back, but she doubted that he heard her. Then she found her way to her room and stripped everything from her bed. It was obvious that she wouldn't be using it tonight, she told herself as she started back to him. She wouldn't dare leave him; she didn't want to leave him. She hated leaving him for even these few minutes.

She'd have to sort out how she really felt some other time. At the moment, she was dealing with a different set of priorities, ones which had nothing to do with how she felt about Simon, or what he had done to her, or the story.

Good lord, the story, she remembered with a start. She hadn't thought of the story since Simon had walked in the door of the hotel. She wondered what Tim would think of his theory of a psychological edge right now. He'd suggested that she might be the one familiar face, and that would help her in getting her interview. He couldn't know how right he'd been about that! She took a wrong turn in the darkened hall and had to retrace her steps, wishing she hadn't thought of Tim, or the interview, or the psychological edge. It seemed unworthy, unfair to Simon and something she couldn't deal with now.

It seemed even less worthy when she re-entered his room and saw his expression. He was quiet again, no longer shaking, and there was something like relief in his eyes when he saw her.

'I thought you'd left,' he remarked idly, his eyes following her as she came towards the bed.

'Only to get more blankets,' she explained, beginning to pile them on him.

'That's a good idea.' He nodded, settling a little more comfortably against the pillow. 'Much better, in fact. Would you turn off the light?' he asked politely, once she had finished with the blankets.

She did and then stood in the darkness, wondering what she ought to do next.

'I've been wanting this for weeks,' he remarked after a moment, his voice drifting lightly. 'A proper bed. You offered me one once—do you remember?'

'Yes,' she said carefully, trying not to remember too much.

'I've been dreaming about a proper bed,' he continued. 'It must be a sign that I'm getting old, or going soft. But there wasn't anything else to dream about,' he added obscurely, and she could hear him shifting restlessly under the covers. 'Victoria, are you still here?' he asked more clearly.

'Yes.'

'Well, do you suppose you could be where I'll know you're here?'

'If you like.' In the dark, she felt for the chair and pulled it to the side of the bed and sat down. For an instant, she debated taking his hand and then decided against it for reasons she didn't attempt to analyse. 'I'm right here,' she told him.

'I know. I thought I wanted to be alone tonight, but I was wrong. Wrong about a lot of things,' he added hastily as he began to shiver uncontrollably again.

It seemed to go on forever, a terrifying sound in the darkness. Finally it ended and she heard his long sigh before his breathing was instantly deep and regular. Well, sleep's probably the best thing, she thought, realising that she didn't have any idea what the best thing might be. The hospital would have been the best thing, but she was stuck with him for the night. In the morning she'd figure out some way to get him to the hospital.

For a long while—she had no idea how long—he slept quietly and then began to turn restlessly from side to side.

'I didn't mean to take so long,' he suddenly said, his voice strained. 'I said three months, and it's been so much longer. I didn't think you'd understand.' He withdrew one arm from beneath the covers and fumbled in the darkness until he found her hand. 'You were so sure I wouldn't come back, and I was so sure I would.'

He sounded delirious, the words tumbling raggedly

over each other as he gripped her hand. He'd forgotten five years, she realised, feeing sick and cold as he continued.

'First we got cut off, you see, and then they found us. And the time was already running short, which is why they found us. I was taking chances—trying to get out—and you can't take chances at a time like that. They questioned me. They kept questioning me.' He drew a long, shuddering breath which gave her a good idea of exactly what he meant. 'I kept count of the days for as long as I could, and I knew there had been too many. That made it worse.' He stirred restlessly. 'Thinking about you had helped, but it went on so long that I was afraid you wouldn't believe me.

'I began to forget,' he continued after a moment, all the hectic energy gone from his voice, the words slower now. 'It went on and on, and it was hard to remember anything. In fact, I don't. I don't remember if they let me go, or if I got away. I don't remember how I got here.'

He hesitated for an instant, suddenly very still. '*Did* I get here?' he asked carefully, gripping her hand more tightly. 'Or is it just imagination?'

'It's not imagination,' she said clearly, returning the pressure of his hand.

'It doesn't feel like imagination,' he agreed thoughtfully, his words a little blurred. 'Your hand feels real enough. So does my leg, come to that. It hurts like hell. If this were a dream, I'd have done away with that, wouldn't I?'

'I expect you would.'

'Well.' He sighed. 'That's good to know. They must have done something to it—my leg, that is.'

'It's broken,' Victoria explained.

'Ah.' He digested that fact for a moment. 'I don't

remember that either, but it's a small price to pay for reality.'

'I suppose so,' she agreed, wondering how or when she would be able to deal with all of this.

'And you didn't stop believing,' he continued, clearly drifting now. 'That's remarkable. I really thought you would.'

His words tore her apart. A while ago, she'd felt unworthy, but there wasn't any way to describe how she felt right now.

'You were so angry when I left,' he said after a long pause. 'I was, too—that you wouldn't trust me. But you did, so that doesn't matter any longer, does it?'

'No.' She leaned her head wearily against the edge of the bed, wishing he'd stop before she completely lost her self-control.

'Thank God for that.' He sighed and then he did stop, immediately asleep.

Victoria came awake to the muezzin's call at dawn, stiff and cold. She lifted her head from the edge of the bed and realised that Simon was already awake and watching her. He still looked grey beneath his tan and his features were still worn and drawn, but the unnatural flush of the fever was gone.

'I've made something of a mistake,' he said quietly as she straightened up, disengaging her hand from his to absently rub at the ache in her back. 'I've been working it out for the last hour or so,' he continued, sounding completely coherent now. 'I was confused last night—to say the least. I had us in a different time and place. I'd left out five years and got it all wrong, hadn't I?'

She nodded, refusing to meet his eyes. She could not deal with this yet, she thought rebelliously. He might be coherent now, but she wasn't. It wasn't fair that he should have managed to work things out while she was still dealing with random fragments—feelings she couldn't handle, too much exposure to the man she'd known five years ago, and a situation which had been completely beyond her control. Right now she didn't know what to do, or say, or even think about the last few hours.

'I still don't understand why you're here,' he said with complete detachment. 'That's what confused me in the first place. And it didn't help when you said—at some point during the night—that you'd been waiting for me. We both know that isn't true. You quit waiting for me over four years ago, didn't you?'

At the moment, she couldn't think of any way to answer that question. He was right that she'd quit waiting for him years ago. Then she'd come to Peshawar to wait for him again, for completely different reasons. But the idea of trying to explain all that was more than she could handle.

'You haven't had much to say for yourself,' he remarked after a few minutes. 'I'd think you were nothing but my imagination working overtime, except that I'm very good at distinguishing reality from illusion. Parts of last night were a rare exception,' he mused, more to himself than to her. 'But that's over now, and you're real enough. And here for a reason, aren't you?' he asked so quickly that he caught her off guard.

'Of course not,' she said defensively and saw his brief expression of disbelief—almost distaste—before his face became expressionless again.

'Of course not,' he agreed mildly. 'Nothing but an amazing coincidence. Tell me—did you ever marry him?'

'Marry who?' she asked, completely confused by his sudden shift. 'Whom?' she corrected without thinking.

'I don't know what his name was,' he pointed out

reasonably. 'You didn't bother to tell me, and I saw no need to ask.'

'Whose name?' She shook her head distractedly, wondering which of them were mad.

'You obviously didn't,' he said with something like amusement in his voice. 'You'd remember, if you had.'

Suddenly, through the haze and confusion, she remembered the last time she'd seen him—the time when she'd lied to him, just to hurt him as much as he'd hurt her. 'That was a mistake,' she began uneasily, wondering how she could begin to explain it to him. For over four years, she had believed that he hadn't really cared, that he'd come back only to continue to toy with her emotions. It hadn't been until sometime during the night that she'd finally learned the truth. 'I had it all wrong,' she began again, but he cut her off.

'Of course,' he agreed evenly. 'You were mad to even consider it. Not to flatter myself, but you'd only have been doing it on the rebound. You weren't ready to marry anyone that soon, Victoria.'

'It wasn't that at all,' she tried again, but he didn't appear to hear her at all.

'I expect you decided a career would be more to your liking,' he said with a trace of sarcasm. 'Still with *Global News*, which has got a marvellous ring to it. It's certainly global enough to get you to northwest Pakistan.' That thought seemed to amuse him. 'That's why you're here, isn't it? You were telling the truth when you said you were waiting for me. You decided I was a story—God knows why—and you were waiting for your story to come back across the border.'

'I was,' she admitted helplessly, trying to meet his eyes and failing miserably. 'But that was before——'

'Spare me the excuses,' he said without expression. 'I expect you're prepared to tell me almost anything you think I want to hear, if it will help you get your story.'

'That's not true!'

'Perhaps you thought I'd be indiscreet again, and tell you even more about my life,' he continued casually. 'Did you think I was still madly in love with you? I'm not, you know, and I'm not about to be indiscreet again. So you're wasting your time,' he finished abruptly.

'But I didn't understand,' she began hesitantly, trying to collect her thoughts and present something approaching a rational explanation. 'Why I came back isn't quite as bad as you think. Nearly as bad, I suppose,' she admitted honestly, 'but it wasn't as though I thought you'd fall into my arms. I thought I'd have something of an advantage—you'd be curious, and I'd be a familiar face. Something like that, anyway,' she continued disjointedly. 'I just wanted an interview. Once I knew you were Peter Soule——'

'What on earth does Peter Soule have to do with me?' Simon asked with a trace of humour—humour at her expense, she could tell. 'Have you come up with some wild idea that I'm Peter Soule?'

'It's not some wild idea! You know perfectly well that you are,' she snapped, momentarily diverted.

'But I'm not,' he said mildly. 'I can't imagine why you think I am.'

'But that's not the point,' she protested, making an effort to get back to what really mattered. 'That's why I came, but then—last night—I found out how wrong I'd been. I don't know how you can forgive me for being so wrong,' she finished miserably.

'What makes you think I want to?' he asked with merely clinical interest. 'I haven't any interest in forgiving you. I haven't any interest in you at all.'

'I don't believe that,' she said carefully. 'You were glad to have me here last night.'

'But that was the fever,' he explained patiently.

'Obviously, you did matter to me in the past, but that ended a long time ago.'

'But feelings just don't change like that,' she protested.

'Of course they do. You ought to be able to understand that—yours have, too. The only difference between us is that mine changed some years ago, while yours seem to have undergone a remarkable metamorphosis between last night and this morning.'

'Because I didn't understand,' she tried again.

His eyes flickered coolly across her face. 'Is it really that, I wonder, or is it that you think you've found the perfect way to get a story? One that doesn't even exist, I might add, except in your imagination. You're wasting your time on two counts, Victoria,' he told her with an empty smile as he pushed himself up and then threw back the blankets. 'There isn't any story—sorry to disappoint you about that—and I don't believe your sudden change of heart. It's years since I'd have believed anything you told me.' He turned to sit on the edge of the bed, favouring his left leg as he did so. 'I'm over you, thank God. I've been over you for years.'

'It can't be over,' she whispered unhappily, unable to accept his words. She'd been loving him since the first moment she'd seen him the night before—not understanding it completely and refusing to accept it, but loving him no less. It was all suddenly clear in her mind. 'It can't be over,' she tried again. 'Not after all we meant to each other.'

'Oh, yes.' He nodded with an icy smile. 'That's a line I tried once on you, and you weren't any more willing to believe it than I am now.' He hesitated for an instant and then used the head of the bed for leverage as he got to his feet. 'You're an unprincipled opportunist, Victoria,' he continued, towering over her, his face livid with anger just barely held in check. 'Five years ago, you wanted me and you were prepared to do anything to have me. Then, when you found you couldn't have me on precisely your own terms, you wrote me out of your life.'

'That's not true——'

'You found someone to better suit your purpose—until you decided that you wanted your precious career even more. Then you wrote him out of your life as easily as I'd been written out. And you've had your precious career, haven't you?' he continued cruelly. 'I've seen your by-line on occasion, these past couple of years. You're moving up in the world. That must please you.

'But nothing would please you more than the story you think I am. You'd love to prove that I'm Peter Soule. As insane as that is, you think it's true, and you'd do anything to get the story. You'd tell me that you didn't understand, swear undying love—anything at all. You're such an opportunist that I expect you'd seduce me, if you thought it would help,' he finished savagely.

'You flatter yourself,' she said coldly, finally goaded to retaliate as his words began to penetrate. 'I wouldn't let you touch me!'

'You've got it all wrong,' he told her, each word clipped and distinct as he leaned over her. 'I have absolutely no interest in touching you. You disgust me.' Abruptly, he turned and took a few experimental steps, pain flickering briefly across his face before his features assumed a set and rigid expression.

'Where do you think you're going?' she demanded, getting to her feet.

'Away from you! It's what I ought to have done the moment I saw you—and spared myself this exposure to your sordid attempts to find a filthy story where none exists.'

'But it does exist,' she called after him, as he started for the door. 'You and I both know it does, and I'll get it! You call *me* an opportunist, but I'll tell the world about the bastard opportunist who uses other people's wars to meet his needs!'

He turned quickly, and she saw the naked anger in his face at the same moment she realised what she'd just said. Five years ago, he'd used that word, and she'd surprised them both with her vehemence when she told him never to say it again. Now she'd just thrown it back at him and she felt an instant's remorse, until he spoke.

'That's nicely put, Victoria,' he said, his voice beyond fury now. 'I don't need reminding to know what *I* am, but you've just done a marvellous job of showing me what *you* are!'

'I don't care what you think of me,' she hurled after him, 'and I'll do anything I can to you—Peter Soule!' She finished triumphantly, knowing that Peter Soule was the one way she had to hurt him.

She didn't think he'd even heard the last of what she'd said. He was already out the door, his halting footsteps retreating down the corridor. But it didn't matter if he heard her now. He'd hear soon enough. She'd make sure she destroyed his precious world—and him.

CHAPTER SEVEN

VICTORIA wasted a fair bit of time considering exactly what she would do to destroy Simon Durant. Once he had had been her knight-errant and—God help her—she had loved him. Then, over the past few weeks, she thought she had succeeded in putting him in perspective. She believed that he'd become an abstraction, nothing but a good story, but she'd been wrong. When he had come back into her life last night, he had proved conclusively that he was neither.

For a while, in the grip of the fever, he had been her knight-errant again—or so she had thought. Only with the clear light of day had she been able to see him for what he really was: unprincipled, cruel, and completely without emotion. He had refused to give her any chance to explain her actions; he hadn't wanted to think anything but the worst of her, and he had certainly succeeded. He'd called her sordid and had said she disgusted him. That was, of course, exactly what he had to believe; he had to think the very worst of her—anything to preserve his precious isolation, to protect himself from feeling anything for her.

She had been prepared to love him again; perhaps she had until he struck back at her in the cruellest possible way. Now she would never forgive him for what he'd said and what he believed about her. He wasn't an abstraction any more; he'd become a personal vendetta. She *would* do everything she could to destroy him. Nothing less would satisfy her, she decided with icy determination.

Then it suddenly came to her that she was being self-indulgent. It was all very well to dwell on Simon Durant and his manifest failings, but she had let him get away while she did so. Fool that she was, she had let him walk out on her when she ought to have followed him. It was vital that she stick to him, dog him unmercifully, and learn everything she could. Now, to learn where Simon had gone, she'd need Rahim's help, and she waited impatiently until he appeared in the hotel lobby.

When he arrived, she gave him the briefest of explanations, saying only that Simon had arrived during the night, that she had seen him before he left again, and now she needed to know where he had gone. Having heard her through, Rahim went immediately to discuss the matter with the desk clerk while Victoria waited beside him. She still didn't understand a word of the language, but it was obvious that Rahim was getting the answers without any difficulty. The clerk appeared pleased to volunteer information, managing to talk non-stop with Rahim while occasionally casting curious glances at Victoria as he did so.

When Rahim turned back to her, she crossed her fingers, hoping to hear that Simon had gone to the hospital. If he had decided to leave the country immediately, he already had a good two hour's lead on them. He could be well on his way to Islamabad by this time, and she was terrified that he might get a flight before she could catch up with him.

'Well,' Rahim began, looking mildly confused and just a little curious, 'he has gone to the Red Cross Hospital, with the two tribesmen who accompanied him here last night. The clerk says you met them when they came in.' He fixed her with an enquiring look.

'Not met them exactly,' she explained, breathing a sigh of relief that Simon was still within reach. 'I just happened to be in the lobby.'

'And I understand now why you were so concerned and anxious,' Rahim continued more kindly. 'You must be very relieved to have him back, although I don't quite understand why he didn't explain to you where he was going. I hadn't realised that you were his wife,' he added when she merely stared blankly at him. 'You hadn't said.'

'His what?' Victoria asked, and then repeated stupidly, 'His what?'

'His wife,' Rahim supplied patiently. 'The clerk says that it is already the talk here—that you are the American's wife. I understand, now, that the idea of an interview was——' he hesitated for an instant, obviously searching for the right words '—a polite fiction, perhaps one would say. And a very good one.' He nodded approvingly. 'So as not to cause a great deal of talk in advance, perhaps.'

'Why on earth would anyone think that I was his wife?' Victoria demanded, shaking her head in confusion.

'But Mr Durant explained it to the tribesmen,' Rahim said simply. 'The clerk on duty at the time heard him. The tribesmen wanted Mr Durant to go to the hospital immediately—they felt he was too ill to delay. But when Mr Durant saw you, he asked that they allow him a few hours with his wife before——'

'That's mad! *He's* mad!' Victoria snapped. 'The whole thing is mad,' she finished explosively.

'Then he is not your husband?' Rahim asked uncertainly, trying to work the matter through.

'Of course he's not!' Victoria was furious, hating the thought that Simon had said such a thing, even in the grip of his fever—for she could only suppose that it had been the fever. But fever or not, it seemed an obscene kind of joke, one more thing to hold against him. 'I expect he'd say almost anything, to be able to do as he pleases,' she added coldly. 'That's the sort of man he is.'

'Perhaps I don't quite understand,' Rahim said doubtfully.

'It doesn't really matter,' she told him impatiently. 'There's no sense in trying to understand a man like that. And I want to go to the Red Cross Hospital now. I need to find out how long he's going to be there, so I'll know when I can see him. For an interview and nothing more,' she finished firmly in the face of Rahim's uncomprehending stare.

At the hospital, they spent an interminable length of time waiting in a crowded corridor while Rahim attempted to learn something about Simon. Victoria lived on nerve, dreading to hear that he'd been seen and immediately released and was now well on his way to Islamabad. Rahim finally produced a doctor; best of all, he was a Westerner, someone she could question directly.

But it wasn't quite that simple. The doctor, an earnest young man, was French, with only a few words of English. Victoria found herself forced back on her three years of college French. It wasn't the most satisfactory arrangement, but she got a reasonably complete explanation as the doctor supplemented his words with plenty of gestures which helped a great deal. He was willing to explain things in detail, once she had produced her press credentials and the information that she was a friend of Monsieur Durant. Not that she was, she thought with grim humour, but she was prepared to say so, if only to retaliate for the fact that he'd had the nerve to call her his wife!

'He is ill,' the doctor began, 'and also wounded in the leg. But it is not as serious as it might seem.' He paused expectantly, to be sure that she understood, and she nodded her comprehension. 'We can take care of the malaria within two or three days, so that he will not feel so ill.

'The leg is another matter,' the doctor continued carefully. 'Not good at all, although it certainly does not threaten his life. There is infection from the wounds, and shrapnel which must be removed. There is also the break which must be set properly. Even surgically reset, I think.'

It took a bit of effort for Victoria to understand this part of it. They were moving into medical terms, and college French was no help with those. The doctor had to try several times, before she could follow him.

'We could handle it here,' the doctor finally continued, 'but not as well, to be honest, as some other hospitals could. It would also take time, which M Durant says he does not have. He says he must return to the United States as soon as possible.'

'How soon?' Victoria demanded, caring a great deal more about Simon's travel plans than his physical condition.

'Tomorrow, he says.' The doctor smiled broadly at the thought. 'But it will be longer than that. A week, perhaps, until the infection is under control. Then he could travel, I think, although it would not be comfortable for him. But M Durant is an exceptional man, is he not? Comfort is obviously not one of his considerations.'

'I don't suppose it is,' Victoria said carefully, avoiding any thought of Simon as an exceptional man. Besides, what mattered most was that she now knew when he would be leaving the hospital, and she would be waiting for him, when he did. She knew very well the length of the trip back to New York, and she'd manage to haunt him all the way. It wouldn't be an easy trip for a man—even an exceptional man—who had been ill and would be uncomfortable. He wouldn't be able to keep up his guard all the time, and she'd be there when he let it slip.

In the end, she nearly wasn't there. She and Rahim spent the next four days talking to as many of the returning guerrillas as possible, attempting to piece together Simon's activities in Afghanistan. It seemed a mere formality to stop at the hospital each morning, to check on Simon's progress. But it was on the fifth morning that they discovered that he had left.

'Only an hour ago,' Rahim soothed, when he saw Victoria's dismay. 'And the driver of his car was instructed to go slowly, because of his leg. We should assume that he will go directly to the airport in Islamabad, but I can have you there nearly as soon as he arrives. Unless he is very fortunate in obtaining a flight, you should still find him there.'

They made it, but only barely, after a mad scramble to collect her things at the hotel and then an even wilder ride down from the highlands into Islamabad. At the airport, they found a flight to Karachi about to leave, and Simon's unmistakeable figure—taller than any other—among the crowd preparing to board. There was a second mad scramble, this time to get Victoria a ticket. After that, there was only a brief opportunity to thank Rahim for his assistance and say goodbye before she began to push through the waiting crowd until she was standing immediately behind Simon.

He had his back to her and was standing, immobile, on a pair of crutches. She didn't think he'd turn to notice her; he seemed oblivious to the crowd around him. She knew that seats on this flight were unreserved, so all she had to do was stay behind him and hope that the seat he chose would be next to an unoccupied one. When the crowd began to surge forward, she followed him on to the plane, hardly daring to breathe. To her relief, he chose a window seat and she moved quickly into the space beside him before he saw her.

When he did, he swore softly under his breath as he started to sit down. Then he straightened up again, as though wondering if he could manage to get past her into the aisle and to another seat.

'I'm not going to move, you know,' she said firmly, blocking the narrow space.

'What in God's name are you doing here?' he demanded savagely, but he did carefully lower himself into his seat.

'I'm after my story—remember?' She smiled with satisfaction as she sat down next to him. 'We've got hours to spend together, between here and New York. You're bound to let something slip in all that time.'

'What makes you think I'm even going to New York?' he asked, the anger in his voice now replaced by weariness.

'That's merely an assumption,' she explained, 'but I've got good at them, these last few years. And it really doesn't matter where you're going. I'll follow you.'

'You'll try, at any rate. Don't be so sure that you'll succeed.'

'I'll succeed,' she told him with complete confidence. 'You may dislike me as much as you please, but I'm very good at sticking with someone—when I'm after an interview.'

'There isn't going to be an interview, and dislike is far too mild a word,' he murmured distastefully, settling back into his seat and closing his eyes.

She took the opportunity to study him more closely. This was the first time she had seen him in really good light and she was surprised at the changes which had taken place in his appearance over the last four years. There were a few streaks of grey in his dark hair now, and his face was thinner and even more worn. At the moment, he didn't look good at all; he was pale beneath his tan and his features drawn, as though the last few days in the hospital hadn't been easy for him.

But there were even more fundamental changes to be seen. The planes and angles in his face had been augmented by harsh lines which bracketed his mouth. They appeared to be permanent, indicating cynicism or a certain jaded view of the world. He no longer projected merely an air of remote detachment; he now looked like a person who treated others with sarcastic bitterness. He certainly didn't look like her knight-errant, she realised. He looked like a thoroughly unpleasant person, one people would do well to avoid.

Feeling a little uneasy, she turned away and didn't look at him again until the plane had taken off and they were being served tea. When she did, she found that it was now his turn to be studying her with a considering, almost calculating, expression.

'Victoria Ward, ace reporter, hasn't had much to say for herself,' he remarked idly when he saw her glance.

'Victoria Ward, ace reporter, has plenty of time.' She smiled briefly as she sipped her tea.

'I'm not going to let anything slip, you know,' he continued almost pleasantly. 'Experts have tried and failed.'

'But I don't intend to torture you,' she said gently and saw his quick, questioning look. 'You let that slip the other night,' she explained casually. 'But don't worry—it wasn't any great help to me. Anyone in your line of work is bound to have been tortured on occasion. It's interesting that you don't remember mentioning that you'd been tortured,' she added with a smile.

'I don't believe I used that term,' he said carefully.

'You don't know what you did or didn't say. You can't remember all of it, and you must be wondering what else you happened to let slip. You can't really know how much you told me and how much I still need to find out. That makes it all the more interesting, don't you think?'

'I know I didn't tell you anything about Peter Soule, if that's what you mean,' he said impatiently. 'Peter Soule is a figment of your imagination. I have nothing to do with him, so there's no reason I would have said anything about him.'

'And our being married was a figment of *your* imagination,' she pointed out quickly. 'Yet you managed to say something about that.'

'Simple expediency,' he explained casually, and she was disappointed to see that he clearly remembered that. She'd hoped to catch him off guard again. 'I'd have said the same about any woman who happened to be in the lobby. My two friends were a little too overbearing about wanting me in the hospital, but they could see the logic in my spending the night with my wife. I'd intended to get rid of you as soon as I could,' he added easily. 'I wanted to be alone.'

'That's not the impression you gave.'

'But you caught me with some of my defences down,' he told her, almost as though he were enjoying this exchange. 'Note that I said some—not all. I never let all my defences down,' he added with a grin.

'No one knows that better than I,' she agreed cheerfully. 'You never did. Perhaps you'll let some of them down again. You're certainly being more civil than you were the last time I saw you.'

'I'm making the best of a bad situation,' he explained pleasantly. 'And finding the change in you absolutely fascinating. You've toughened up, Victoria. Got brittle and self-assured. You're not at all the naive little girl I knew five years ago.'

'That's right; I'm not. But you're trying to change the subject.'

'What subject is that?' he asked with an almost appreciative look.

'Peter Soule.'

'Peter Soule doesn't exist.'

'Of course he does. He wrote *Under Starlight* and *A Sure Defeat*.'

'A pseudonym,' Simon said firmly. 'His publisher has made that very clear.'

'*Your* pseudonym,' she answered just as firmly.

'Why on earth would you think a thing like that?'

'You know very well why I'd think a thing like that!'

He nodded. 'I suppose so,' he agreed, as though the issue were of merely academic interest. 'I've told you a fair bit about my life, and you've read his books. You found a few parallels and made the most of them.'

'I found nothing but parallels.'

'But there would be so many—you ought to realise that,' he explained easily. 'We were both doing the same sort of work in the army, after the same sort of training. I wasn't the only man to lead a Special Mission Team, you know. There were a surprising number of us. For all I know,' he continued thoughtfully, 'I've met Peter Soule. I may even have worked with him. I've often wondered about that, but I'm no closer to knowing who he really is than anyone else.'

'That's hard to believe,' Victoria said with a teasing note. 'You ought to know him very well indeed! You were nearly always in the same places at the same time. You must have been tripping over him constantly.'

'Oh, well,' Simon said with a dismissing gesture, 'I've read his books, too, and I think it's safe to say that he took a few liberties with his places and dates.'

'But you didn't,' she said softly. 'Your military

record and *Under Starlight* match beautifully, except where your record is classified. It's a really remarkable coincidence, that *he* should take liberties that are *your* military record. Really remarkable,' she repeated thoughtfully.

'Is it?' he asked unhelpfully and then settled more comfortably in his seat. 'I've had enough of Peter Soule for the moment,' he told her, closing his eyes. 'I'm going to ignore you.'

'You don't sleep on planes,' she objected.

'That's right,' he agreed evenly, and she wondered if he remembered as well as she did when he'd told her that. 'But I'm very good at ignoring people, when it suits my purpose.'

Well, let him ignore her, she decided complacently. They were only an hour from Karachi, and it might better suit *her* purpose if she had more than an hour in which to pursue the subject of Peter Soule. Still ahead of them was the eight-hour flight to Paris, when she would manage to sit with him again. She'd wait until she had him as a captive audience for that long stretch—when he'd be more tired and his resistance lower. Thus far, she felt that things were going very well. At least he was willing to talk to her, and she had the feeling that he was actually enjoying it in a perverse way. He was matching wits with her quite nicely, but the trip had only just started. She was confident that he wasn't—at least right now—the man of iron he thought he was. In the hours to come, his guard was bound to slip. There really was plenty of time, she told herself complacently, and actually slept for a while.

At the airport in Karachi she followed Simon at a distance until she saw him stop at the Air France reservations desk. She waited until he had conducted his business and then went to collect her luggage. By the time she returned, Simon had disappeared in the confusion of the terminal, but she made for Air France and assumed her most engaging smile.

She confided to the clerk that she was travelling with M Durant who had been there only a little while ago to make their reservations. But she was just a little concerned. As the clerk would have seen for himself, M Durant was injured and also ill. 'Un peu délirant,' she added for malicious good measure, finding her French coming more easily after her practice session five days before with the doctor at the Red Cross Hospital. M Durant might well have completely neglected to make *two* reservations—while she was struggling with the baggage and unable to check on him.

The clerk was able to confirm this omission, and understood completely M Durant's otherwise unaccountable lapse. The clerk also understood the need for M Durant's companion to be with him on the plane. In fact, the clerk's admiring glance led Victoria to believe he would have understood M Durant's desire to be with her, even if he were not ill and in need of solicitous attention. The fact that M Durant was a little delirious obviously explained everything to the clerk's satisfaction, and Victoria soon had her reserved seat—next to Simon's.

In first class, too, she noted, grateful that *Global News* was picking up the tab. It seemed that Simon still had his weaknesses, even after all these years. It would be considerably more comfortable than the crowded flight from Islamabad—where there hadn't been any first-class section—and Simon was going to need all the comfort he could find. Their flight was scheduled for ten in the evening, which meant that he had to wait here at the airport for another good three hours and then endure the eight-hour flight to Paris. By the time they arrived, he'd have been up for more than twenty-four hours—fighting jet lag, a broken leg, and infection. At some point during the long night, his guard was bound to come down.

She stayed well behind Simon, during the process of boarding the plane, and it didn't appear that he had seen her. She expected to have an element of surprise working for her, when she slipped into the seat next to his. But she clearly didn't, and she was tempted to slap his face when he smiled blandly up at her from his seat by the window.

'Playing cat and mouse, Victoria?' he asked pleasantly as she sat down beside him. 'You needn't have bothered. I knew you'd be here. I haven't tried my best efforts yet.'

'I'm not sure you've got any left,' she told him, noting that he was beginning to look grey beneath his tan.

'Don't count on that.' His tone was ironic, but she could hear the strain in his voice and he lapsed into a silence which lasted until after the plane had taken off. Then he ordered a double Scotch from the steward and sipped it cautiously.

'Feeling better?' Victoria asked, having waited patiently until about half the drink was gone.

'Infinitely,' he agreed with an easy grin, and it did seem that his colour was better. 'It's nice to know that you can be understanding, on occasion. Or is it that you think one Scotch will be enough?'

'Enough for what?' she asked innocently.

'Enough to make me throw caution to the winds and tell you everything you'd like to know.'

'Will it be?'

'No. Not even two,' he observed dispassionately, finishing his drink and immediately signalling for another. 'You see, Victoria, I'm toying with you,' he continued pleasantly, once he had his second drink in hand. 'This is always a long and tedious trip, and I'm not at my best right now. You're providing an interesting diversion, but it's no use if I don't feel like enjoying it.'

'You'll feel like hell in the morning,' she couldn't resist pointing out.

'Perhaps. But that's hours away, and it will be worth it. How shall we while away the hours?' he asked expectantly.

'Discussing Peter Soule,' she answered promptly.

'Like a broken record.' He sighed, but he didn't seem displeased. 'You will not get that idea out of your head.'

'But you're enjoying it,' she told him. 'You and I both know that's who you are, but you're enjoying all this fencing. You're proving some obscure point to yourself with all of this. I'm not sure what, but it really doesn't matter.'

'Why doesn't it?' he asked with detached interest.

'Because I'm going to get the story anyway. You can't do anything about it.'

'You have changed, haven't you?' he asked pleasantly. 'You've acquired enormous self-confidence, since I last knew you.'

'I've grown up.'

'That, too, of course,' he agreed easily, 'but there's more to it than that. You've become more capable, and that doesn't always come with growing up. You were capable enough to make your way around Peshawar without any difficulty—which is not something I'd expect every American young woman to do.'

'Oh, well, I had help with that,' Victoria explained candidly, realising that she couldn't have managed without Rahim.

'Still, part of being capable is knowing when you *do* need help,' he said approvingly. 'And you've shown considerable ingenuity in sticking with me. I honestly thought I'd seen the last of you, when I left the hospital. I didn't think you'd be able to catch up with me, although I was aware that you were stopping at the hospital each day—to solicitously enquire about my health.' He grinned appreciatively. 'And you've done very well since then, too,' he finished with approval.

'You're being very kind, almost flattering,' she said with a demure smile. 'But you *are* trying to change the subject.'

'Ah yes, you'd like to get back to this harebrained idea of yours about a story.'

'But it's not harebrained, and there *is* going to be a story,' she explained, attempting to be reasonable. 'It would be a better story—a more balanced one—if you'd co-operate.'

'And I'm supposed to want to give you a better story—a more balanced one?' He smiled sceptically.

'Better for *you*,' she said quickly.

'By leaving out some of the more embarrassing details?' he asked with idle curiosity. 'Are you suggestng that you'd omit some of the things Peter Soule has chosen to avoid?'

'I could,' she agreed carefully, trying not to let her excitement show. It didn't matter whether it was her argument or the Scotch, but she had the feeling that he was wavering slightly. 'I might,' she added softly.

'Then let's suppose,' he began conversationally, pausing long enough to take another drink, 'that I am Peter Soule. You'll notice that I only said "suppose"—but, if I were, do you mean that there are things you might leave out? You see, there are some things you know about me that I might not want the rest of the world to know—*if* I were Peter Soule.

'There was a time, with you, when I was far too indiscreet,' he continued almost casually. 'I told you things I'd never told anyone else, before or since. I'm not sure why, except that you had a way about you.' He hesitated for an instant, looking puzzled or confused. 'But that's beside the point,' he hurried on. 'The fact remains that there are things you know, things that I'd rather other people didn't—*if* I were Peter Soule. As you so succinctly put it the other night, there's the way I've used other people's wars to meet my needs. That's hardly noble, is it? It doesn't suit Peter Soule's image in the least.' For a few moments he stared uncomfortably down into the contents of his glass. 'And then there are the circumstances of my birth,' he finally continued with a twisted smile. 'Another point you managed to make the other night. Or was it morning by that time?' he asked, momentarily diverted as he looked up at her.

'I think it was morning by then,' she answered carefully.

'No matter.' He gestured dismissively. 'That's not the point, is it? The point is that Peter Soule wouldn't want the world to know about that. Imagine the fun the press would have with it! Of course, you're a part of the press,' he said parenthetically, 'but I'm thinking about the rest of them. Peter Soule—that fine and idealistic young man—except he's not so young as he used to be,' Simon mused lightly. 'He's nearly forty now, a bit too old for youthful idealism. But everybody thinks of Peter Soule as young and idealistic, and bastard status would tend to dim the lustre, wouldn't it?' he finished bleakly.

'That doesn't have to be a part of the story,' Victoria said softly.

'Better if it's not. It ruins his image completely, I think, if the world knows he's a bastard.'

Here it comes, Victoria told herself, watching as Simon stared into his glass for an instant before draining it. It's about to happen now.

'And if I were Peter Soule,' Simon resumed,

surprising her completely because his voice was suddenly crisp and assured, 'I wouldn't want you to ruin his image, would I? I'd do almost anything to protect it, I expect—even to the point of co-operating with you. But I'm not Peter Soule,' he continued with a curious smile. 'I don't give a damn about his image, and I'm certainly not interested in co-operating with you— not for any reason.

'I don't even like Peter Soule. I've read his books, and he's self-indulgent. He bares his soul far more than any man should—that's undoutedly where he gets his pseudonym. He's a bore and a braggart—always going off to tilt at other people's windmills and then coming back to capitalise on what he's done by writing a book about it. I don't like Peter Soule,' he said again, with distaste. 'I don't care what you write about Peter Soule. You may write anything you please. You may do your best to prove that he and I are the same person, but I'll deny it by saying nothing at all. That's what others have done, when the press has set out to prove that any one of them was Peter Soule. You can do your best to make me into Peter Soule, but it won't work. It will be nothing more than a nine day's wonder, like all the rest.

'The story will die,' he continued cheerfully, 'and you'll simply be just one more reporter who tried to have a shot at that particular guessing game and fell flat on—in this case—*her* face. And I think I've left you speechless,' he observed after a moment. 'That must be some kind of a first for the new and improved Victoria Ward! I wish you could see the expression on your face,' he finished with a self-satisfied smile.

'I think you're mad,' was all she could find to say because he'd taken her so completely by surprise.

'I'm sure you do,' he agreed easily. 'Perhaps you've even told me so before. We've hurled so many recriminations at each other through the years—that must have been one of them. And feel free to think me mad, if it pleases you. Think anything you like,' he offered generously.

'This has been nothing but a game to you,' she burst out bitterly.

'That's right. I told you so at the start. Actually, what I said was that I was toying with you,' he corrected carefully. 'Years ago, you accused me of doing just that. As it happened, I wasn't, but you wouldn't believe me. I thought it might be interesting to try it now, and it has been.' He nodded approvingly.

'It was nothing but revenge,' she whispered.

'No. Not revenge,' he said, sounding suddenly weary. 'I'm too old for revenge. I'm too old to even care. It's been years since I've cared about much of anything.' Abruptly, he signalled the steward for another drink. 'All I ask now is a little diversion,' he continued almost absently, when the glass had been placed before him. 'It really doesn't matter what. A war in Afghanistan or a couple of hours with you—they're all very much the same, except that some things occupy more time than others. Nothing matters any more,' he said quietly, more to himself than to her. 'I don't even care, as long as it kills some time. And there's always too much time to be killed.' He was silent for a few moments, staring down at the glass.

'But I do owe you that much, I suppose.' He roused slightly, lifting his glass to her in a silent salute. 'You've provided a little diversion. That's all I ask now,' he repeated carefully, draining the glass and then setting it down a little unsteadily. 'That and a little sleep,' he added uncertainly. 'Between you and the Scotch, I might just manage that, too.'

Perhaps he did; Victoria couldn't be sure. He leaned back in his seat, eyes closed, but she didn't know whether he was sleeping or had simply retreated from everything.

What have we done to each other? she asked herself over and over through the long hours of the flight. What have we done? The other night—the other morning, she corrected automatically—she'd been furious with him because he wouldn't listen to her attempts to explain. But that hadn't been any different than the time she'd refused to hear his explanation, when he had finally come back to her.

As he'd said, they'd hurled so many recriminations at each other through the years. Even during the years apart, the bitterness had been growing; they'd never stopped blaming each other for the way they had each destroyed their love. She knew very well what it had done to her. It had made her brittle, and left her caring about nothing but her career. She'd cut out all human relationships and hadn't allowed herself to care about anyone. Except, she reminded herself, for those few short hours after Simon had materialised in the lobby of the hotel in Peshawar. She had cared about him then.

But what the bitterness had done to Simon was even worse. She had been so successful in her attempts to hurt him that she had left him empty, unable to care about anything except killing time. For an instant, she had seen it clearly. He had let his guard down, but not in the way she had expected or thought she wanted. Instead of seeing Peter Soule—and she wondered now why she'd ever cared about Peter Soule—she'd had a glimpse of Simon. What she had seen had been terrifying—the terrible isolation of having nothing to do but kill time.

And she had to do something about it, she told herself with an emotion which was somewhere between panic and resolve. She had to reach him and find some way to undo the damage she'd done so many years before. If it wasn't too late, she bleakly reminded herself. If she still could.

CHAPTER EIGHT

VICTORIA lost Simon completely in Paris. She took it for granted that he would again use Air France, so she didn't bother to follow him, but had immediately gone to claim her luggage. When she finally got to the Air France counter, she felt her first hint of concern as the clerk assured her that there had been no recent reservation by a M Durant.

She was forced to go from airline to airline, meeting with negative shakes of the head each time she explained her story in her careful French. She was fighting a real sense of panic now, because she seemed to have lost Simon completely. He'd warned her that he hadn't tried his best efforts, but now it seemed that he had. They seemed to have been all too successful, and she was driven by the dreadful certainty that she'd never find him, if she didn't find him now.

She never knew how she happened to think of the airport hotel, but she did, hoping that Simon would have thought of it, too. It finally seemed the only logical alternative; if Simon had felt as bad as he looked, when he left the plane without speaking to her, he'd have needed a good rest. She couldn't believe her luck when the room clerk was more than helpful. He remembered M Durant—' *parfaitement*'. And he could understand why M Durant's illness would cause him to neglect to register for both himself and his charming companion.

Within a short period of time, Victoria was presented with a second key to the room. Only then was she faced with the disturbing realisation that she had no idea of what she would say, now that she was about to face Simon. She could hardly announce that it had come to her, during the night, that the two of them had spent five years destroying each other's lives and that it was time for them to stop. After twenty-four hours without sleep, she wasn't up to that kind of conversation, and Simon would be less able to handle it than she.

When she finally let herself nervously into the room, she found that she wasn't going to have to do or say anything for quite some time. One dim light was on in the room, but it was enough to show her precisely how things were. Simon had carelessly dropped his clothing on the floor, with the crutches beside them. He was sound asleep in the bed nearest the door. Dead to the world was more like it, she thought dispassionately, noting the open vial of pain pills and the glass of water on the table beside the bed. Simon wasn't going anywhere for at least a few hours; he wasn't even going to know she was in the room.

She took a shower, washed her hair and then changed into the uncrushable peasant dress she'd had the foresight to tuck into her flight bag. When she returned to the bedroom, she found that Simon hadn't moved during her absence. His face was oddly shadowed by the light, his left profile clearly showing the ravages of the trip while his right revealed nothing. He was obviously going to sleep for some time and Victoria saw no reason why she shouldn't take the other bed and have a nap. As a precaution, in case he awoke before she did, she hunted silently through his things until she found his passport and his wallet. She slipped them into the wide pocket of her dress and then settled on the other bed.

For a while, she didn't sleep, but lay there, watching the shadow of Simon's form and trying to work out what she would finally say to him. But nothing seemed to come, except for an overwhelming sense of longing to make things right. She didn't seem able to translate that longing into words, so she finally gave up and went to sleep.

When she woke up, it took a little time to work out where she was, and why. When she had, her eyes went instantly to the other bed, and she drew a silent sigh of relief when she saw that he was still there. It appeared that he was still as sound asleep as before. He'd clearly been at the end of his endurance, she thought with a sense of remorse, remembering the way she'd intended to use that against him. While he looked a little better now, she hoped that he'd sleep for as long as he could.

When she checked her watch, she saw that nearly eight hours had passed. She also realised that she was starving and definitely in need of coffee to clear her brain. So she left the room, keeping his wallet and passport with her, to have a quick lunch in the hotel's coffee shop before returning to the room.

When she silently unlocked the door and let herself in, she found herself facing an entirely different set of circumstances. Simon was up. He had showered and shaved, and now he sat on the edge of the bed, with nothing but a towel wrapped around his waist. He hadn't heard her enter the room, so she stood watching while he shook two of the pain pills into his hand and then swallowed them with water. It was only when he reached carefully for the flight bag beside the bed that she saw his slight hesitation before he looked up at her.

'I won't even ask,' he said with resignation. 'I honestly thought I'd lost you, this time.' He closed his eyes for a moment and then opened them, staring at her with something like active dislike. 'There must be a word for someone like you, but I can't think what it is at the moment.'

'Unprincipled opportunist,' she suggested, watching while he drew the flight bag on to the bed.

'That will do,' he agreed absently, beginning to hunt through the contents of the bag, removing some small boxes and packages with hands that trembled slightly. While he looked more rested, his features were so rigidly set that she suspected he was in considerable pain. She supposed that her sudden appearance hadn't helped in the least.

'What are you trying to do?' she asked after a moment, not moving from where she stood by the door.

'Trying to see to my leg,' he explained, looking through the collection of things beside him, as though trying to make some sense of them.

She nodded, her eyes drawn instantly to his left leg. The doctor in Peshawar had mentioned shrapnel wounds, and Victoria only now understood what that meant. His leg was difficult to look at, marked with small incisions and red angry wounds running from just below his knee to his ankle. 'Are you sure you can manage?' she asked anxiously as he swung his leg up on to the bed.

'I can manage anything,' he said briefly, fumbling with a packet of gauze squares for a moment and then letting it fall. 'But not for a minute or two,' he added to himself. 'It can wait.' He lowered himself down on to the pillow and closed his eyes. 'This all seemed like a fine idea,' he finally continued, apparently for her benefit. 'I decided it might be pleasant to feel like a human being again, but I should have left well enough alone. I don't think I can put it all back together again.' He smiled briefly, as though he found the thought vaguely amusing.

'I'll do it,' she said with sudden resolution. 'I've taken a first aid course.'

'Did it cover shrapnel wounds?' he asked with idle

curiosity, but he didn't resist as she set to work. 'I should think they'd be a little too out of the ordinary.'

'The principle ought to be the same,' she answered steadily, forcing herself to ignore the way his hand suddenly gripped the sheet as she applied antiseptic to the wounds. 'I'm sorry that it has to hurt for a bit.'

'Oh, that's all right. I should think that would be just what you want. Now's the time to ask me anything.' He attempted a grin and didn't quite pull it off. 'I'm bound to let something slip. Possibly everything,' he added with a sigh.

'I don't care about that,' she said without thinking, done with the antiseptic and beginning to cover the wounds with gauze squares.

'Trying some new and devious tack,' he mused. 'Lulling me into a false sense of security, and succeeding remarkably well. You're very gentle.'

'I'm trying.'

'Trying to be gentle, or trying to lull me into a false sense of security?' he asked.

'Trying to be decent for a change,' she snapped, using a roll of gauze to wrap his leg and hold her makeshift job in place. 'There's an elastic bandage here. Am I supposed to use that, too?'

He nodded. 'On top of the rest. Have you ever considered guerrilla warfare, Victoria?' he asked with a sudden shift.

'In what way?' Her tone was distracted as she struggled with the bandage.

'As a guerrilla, of course. You'd make a good one. You've got all the right instincts—begin by doing the unexpected, never lose your nerve, keep at it with dogged determination. I think you've missed your calling, and I've acquired a grudging admiration for you, these past few days, or hours, or whatever it's been.' Something in what he'd just said seemed to amuse him. 'Done so soon?' he asked, as she swept the remains of the supplies back into his flight bag and then carefully pulled the blanket over him.

'If it doesn't fall off,' she said doubtfully.

'It wouldn't dare fall off,' he assured her with a brief smile. 'It feels fine. So do I, come to that.' He raised himself up long enough to rearrange the pillow against the headboard of the bed and then leaned back against it in a half sitting position. 'What now?' he asked with a lazy smile, watching the way she stood awkwardly beside the bed.

'I don't know.' She shook her head nervously, wondering how to begin, or even if she ought to try.

'Now's the time to try to seduce me,' he suggested helpfully, 'if that's what you had in mind.'

'That's *not* what I had in mind!' she snapped, and then drew a breath. 'I came here to try to make things right between us.'

'Now there's a tall order. I can't believe it's possible, and why should you want to, after all these years?'

'Because we've both been miserable for all these years,' she answered defiantly.

'That's true,' he agreed, studying her face with careful deliberation. 'I almost believe you mean it.' He sounded surprised.

'I do.'

'Why the sudden change of heart?' he asked softly, catching her by the hand and pulling her down beside him.

'Because I've finally seen what we've done to each other. What I did to you,' she corrected with scrupulous honesty.

'So you've decided it was all your fault,' he said with a strange smile. 'That doesn't sound like Victoria Ward, ace reporter. That sounds like a girl I knew five years ago.'

'I wish it were five years ago,' she admitted unhappily. 'I wish we could start all over again.'

'Perhaps we can.' She saw the brief flicker of uncertainty in his eyes before it was replaced by a grin which suddenly made him look years younger. 'It might help if we began by letting me kiss you properly. I think I'm in the mood for that, and it's been years since I've kissed you properly.' There was amusement in his voice as he slowly drew her towards him.

'I think we ought to talk,' she objected as firmly as she could, but it was hard to maintain her resolution as he drew her even closer.

'I'd rather kiss you. I've been wanting to for days.' His lips brushed lightly against her forehead. 'Even when I was actively hating you, I was wanting to do this. That doesn't make any sense, does it?'

'Nothing about us makes any sense,' she admitted helplessly as his lips trailed down the side of her face.

'Unless it's that we never stopped loving each other,' he murmured, his lips continuing to taste her skin. 'If that's true, then it all makes perfect sense,' he whispered just before his mouth closed over hers.

It did make perfect sense, she thought dizzily, realising how much she had wanted this as she leaned against him. He kissed her with careful deliberation, teasing and tempting and leaving her hungry for more. She rested her hands lightly against his chest, feeling his heart beat beneath her touch as his mouth became more insistent. Her need answered his as his hands began to caress her and she moved restlessly against him.

The soft folds of her dress were no real barrier as he continued to follow the curves of her body, but she sensed his impatience and willingly submitted when he removed the dress and cast it aside. His hands glided freely on her skin as the last restraints fell away and his touch became more possessive.

'Your leg,' she protested, fighting for rational thought when he turned with her and pulled the blankets back to gather her body into the long line of his.

'My leg's got nothing to do with this,' he murmured, his lips moving against her skin while she clung helplessly to the hard muscles of his back. 'This is marvellous,' he breathed, the weight of his body coming to rest on hers as his lips moved lower to find the valley between her breasts. 'I can't get enough of you. I never could.' He sighed as she cradled his head against her.

'No one else could make me feel like this,' she whispered, her fingers brushing lightly through his hair and then gently kneading the muscles of his shoulders. Her body was alive with the sensation of their closeness, filled with a strange contentment which still left her wanting more. 'I can't imagine doing this with anyone but you,' she heard herself confessing helplessly as her hands teased slowly down his back to caress the lean line of him.

'Ah, Victoria.' He drew an involuntary breath, sounding shaken. 'It's been so long,' he murmured, his lips moving hungrily while she felt a sudden rush of tenderness. 'I didn't know how much I needed you,' he ended with a sigh.

For long moments they lost themselves in shared desire, sensation overwhelming both of them. Tenderness and passion were joined in their need to drive away five years of emptiness, to rediscover what neither of them had been able to forget. Time ceased to exist as their hands and lips explored with infinite care, their bodies on fire with a passion to erase the past.

Gradually, their movements slowed, awareness replacing the aching need which had possessed them both. No words were necessary as their hands grew still and their lips abandoned their hungry explorations. It was silent understanding which caused them to draw slightly away from each other, their bodies only barely touching. For a few minutes they simply looked at each other, and then Victoria saw Simon's slow smile.

'Well,' he said unsteadily, 'some things haven't changed. This hasn't changed.' Absently, he reached out to run his fingers through her curls. 'I'd forgotten quite how much this means to me. *You* mean to me,' he corrected carefully.

'I'd forgotten *everything*,' she burst out, shaken by the force of her response to him.

'Not quite everything,' he teased. 'I'd say you remembered quite a bit. Whatever it was about you that left me always wanting more—you haven't forgotten that.' A curious smile played around the corners of his mouth. 'If you've come here to seduce me, you're off to a marvellous start.'

'That's not why I came.'

'I know.' He nodded slowly. 'I do believe you. I'm prepared to believe anything you say right now.' He smiled again. 'Still, you've missed your chance. I'd have told you anything, a few minutes ago. I expect I still would. You always made me tell you things I'd never said to anyone.'

'I never made you tell me anything,' she objected lazily, comforted by this new understanding between them.

'Of course you did. Or made me want to.' His hand, which had been slowly threading through her hair, was suddenly still. 'Good Lord,' he breathed, a startled look in his eyes. 'We've already had this conversation—five years ago. Do you remember?'

'In the graveyard——'

'That first afternoon,' he finished for her. 'What's happening, Victoria?' he asked unsteadily. 'I'm not sure of this. Is it really possible to leave five years behind? Forget they ever happened?'

'I want it to be,' she said fiercely.

'So do I, I think.' He bent his head to touch his lips to the curve of her shoulder. 'I want you back the way you were five years ago. The way *we* were,' he corrected almost absently as his lips left her skin. He settled back against the pillow, studying her face. 'Do you suppose it's possible?'

Victoria shook her head helplessly, not knowing what to say. She knew what she wanted, but the years of bitterness seemed an almost insurmountable barrier between them.

'You're frightened, aren't you?' he asked gently, one hand smoothing back the curls from her forehead. 'But I don't think you should be. Anything seems possible, now that we're together.'

She leaned her head gratefully against his chest, lulled by the touch of his fingers, threading slowly through her hair. Anything did seem possible at this moment. They were together with a kind of closeness which went beyond physical need. She'd never felt like this before, she decided dreamily, allowing her thoughts to drift. She'd never felt such a sense of peace and security in Simon's arms. She'd always been afraid, always unsure of herself—and of him. But now, suddenly, everything had changed. 'I'm not frightened,' she finally said, her voice coloured by the surprise she felt at having finally lost her fear. 'I'm not a bit afraid,' she said, this time with more conviction.

'Aren't you?'

'No. I always was, you know. I didn't see how you could possibly love me, and I didn't think that anything good would ever last for me. I didn't expect *us* to last. I was always waiting for the whole thing to end, which is why I was always frightened.'

'And now you're not?' he asked carefully.

'No.' She shook her head. 'God knows why, because there's even less reason to expect us to last, this time. How I feel doesn't make any sense.'

'Perhaps it's because you've grown up,' he suggested, his fingers continuing to thread lightly through her hair.

'I expect you're right. I was awfully young, five years ago. Wasn't I?' she asked when he made no reply.

'You were,' he agreed evenly, 'although I didn't realise it at the time. I'd been fooled by my image of Victoria Ward, with all her marvellous serenity and composure.'

'Oh, Lord!' She sighed. 'I wasn't behaving at all like *that* Victoria Ward. I didn't have any serenity and composure where you were concerned. I was all nerves and raw edges, and hopelessly adolescent. I had the most incredible case of hero worship about you,' she explained, lifting her head so she could look at him. 'I *did* love you, but it was all mixed up with too much hero worship. I didn't feel worthy of you, I suppose.'

'And now that I'm battered and worn, and considerably the worse for wear, you don't have any hero worship left,' he suggested with the hint of a smile.

'I wouldn't say that,' she protested, studying his face. 'Although I have to admit that a summer in Afghanistan doesn't seem to have been particularly relaxing.'

'That's the understatement of the year,' he murmured with a quick grin.

'But you're still the most attractive man I've ever known,' she told him. 'You still remind me of a knight-errant; I expect you always will. But it's not hero worship anymore. There's considerably more reality involved this time.'

'There had better be,' he said firmly, 'because there's not going to be any more of this knight-errant business. It may please you to think that's what I am, when I'm off fighting other people's wars, but it's only fair to warn you that I'm not going to be doing it any longer.'

'Aren't you?'

'No. I'm much too old, and I made entirely too many careless mistakes this time. I've had enough of breaking legs and stepping on mines. There's got to be a more comfortable way of earning a living. Sorry to disappoint you,' he added with another quick grin, 'but I'm going to abandon my status as a knight-errant.'

'I never said you had to fight wars to be a knight-errant,' she chided gently. 'I'd decided that's what you were *before* you told me about fighting wars. And I should think you'd be considerably safer if you didn't fight them. Unless you're going to decide to take up something equally dangerous,' she added doubtfully.

'As a matter of fact, I'm going to write,' he explained with a hint of self-consciousness. 'There shouldn't be any danger in that.'

'Are you going to go back to being Peter Soule?' she asked with sudden daring and then instantly wondered if she'd gone too far.

'For God's said, don't start on that again,' he warned, but there wasn't any anger in his voice. In fact, he sounded amused, and there was an expression in his eyes which might have been admiration. 'You don't give up without a struggle, do you?' he asked, and then continued without allowing her to answer. 'Don't spoil things now, just when we're doing so well.'

'I'm sorry,' she began as he caught her off guard and kissed her with slow and careful deliberation. 'I won't bring it up again,' she promised breathlessly when his lips finally left hers.

'That's better,' he said approvingly, gathering her closer. 'You really ought to forget about Peter Soule, you know. Besides, I should think you'd *want* to hear what I've got planned for the rest of my life,' he continued, his fingers returning to her hair, 'particularly as it may well include you. If you're willing,' he added, almost as an after thought.

'I expect I might be,' she agreed lazily, comforted by this new ease between them, and the prospect of a future for them both. 'I'd rather have you writing about wars than fighting in them.'

'Ah—but I'm not going to write about wars,' he corrected. 'I'm going to write about the victims of wars. That seems more suitably knight-errant, don't you think? It's been said that the real victims of guerrilla warfare are the people who aren't fighting for either side—the innocent bystanders who get caught in the middle. I've seen enough to know it's true, so perhaps there's a certain poetic justice to be found in writing about the people who used to be my victims. I should like to make others understand just what happens to the innocent bystanders of this world.

'And there's another thing I should like,' he continued, gathering momentum as he spoke. 'I should like to find an old farm house, somewhere in New Hampshire, I think. It wouldn't hurt if there were an old graveyard in the general area.' He hesitated for an instant and then went on, a faraway note in his voice. 'I've got a particular one in mind, you know. It's hopelessly sentimental, but I should like us to go back to your graveyard, some fine June day. That's where I fell in love with you,' he murmured, his lips against her forehead, 'and I stayed in love with you. That's the surprising thing: that I kept on loving you. I honestly didn't think I had.'

'You didn't act as though you had,' Victoria pointed out with a certain complacency.

'I know.' He nodded. 'But I *liked* you better.'

'Did you?'

'Absolutely. I don't remember much about that night when I came back to the hotel, but by the next morning I realised that you'd improved considerably. Even when we were about as angry with each other as two people can be, I was pleased to see how much you'd improved. At least I was fighting with a woman this time, and not a clinging vine. *That* made for a pleasant change.'

'I was a dreadfully clinging vine five years ago,' she admitted honestly. 'I suppose it was that I hadn't had anything to cling to for so long. At least that's got better.'

'It's more than that,' he corrected almost absently, his lips leaving her forehead to trace the line of her cheek. 'You've toughened up, in the nicest possible way. I expect you could do just about anything, if you put your mind to it. You've done this, after all.'

'Done what?' she asked distractedly as he kissed her lightly.

'Destroyed all my defences again.' His lips moved on to touch the curve of her shoulder. 'But you shouldn't have cut your hair,' he teased as he continued to explore her skin. 'I loved it long and tangled.'

'That's why I cut it off,' she said without thinking. 'It made me remember you and I couldn't bear that. It hurt too much.'

'Damn.' He sighed, the teasing note instantly gone from his voice as he raised his head to look at her. 'We've found so many ways to hurt each other, haven't we?'

'And all my fault,' she admitted miserably.

'It wasn't all your fault,' he corrected gently, 'although it pleased me for a while to think it was. But there was always so much of myself that I wouldn't let you see. Even when I wanted to, there were things I couldn't say, or wouldn't say. It's no wonder that you doubted me.' He hesitated for a moment and then continued uncomfortably. 'If there's blame, we've got to share it equally. That makes this whole thing even more complicated.' The thought seemed to irritate him. 'God knows what we're going to do about it!'

'Can't we just start over?' she asked reasonably.

'Easy enough for you to say,' he complained. 'But I'm not sure I've got the courage to start over.'

'You've got more courage than anyone I know.'

'But it's all the wrong kind.' He stirred uneasily. 'I'm brave about all the wrong things, and I'm an expert at being alone. I always was, but I've become even more accomplished, these last five years.' He tried to smile, but it only served to emphasise the tension in his face. 'I'm not sure I've got the courage to give that up.'

'But you want to,' she coaxed.

'Of course I want to,' he agreed, 'but not if I can't do it properly.'

'I'm willing to make allowances,' she suggested.

'I don't want allowances made,' he said impatiently. 'What I've got to do is think this whole thing through.'

'I don't see what there is to think through,' she objected. 'You love me, don't you?'

'You make it difficult not to.' He smiled briefly, his eyes holding hers.

'And I love you. You see? It's as easy as that.'

'It's not as easy as that.' He sighed wearily. 'It's considerably more difficult.'

'Why?' she asked lightly, determined not to accept any objections.

'Oh Lord, Victoria!' He stirred impatiently. 'For all the same reasons it was difficult five years ago, only they're worse now. *I'm* worse now. I'm no good at caring any more. It's got out of control, these past few years. I actually *like* what I'm doing. I like using other people and fighting other people's wars. Wars are absorbing propositions; I actually enjoy them now. Five years ago, I hated the whole thought of it all, but that's changed now.' He hesitated for a moment and then went on with extreme reluctance. 'I don't even mind the killing. It's become an intellectual exercise—to see how well I can do it. I don't even care about that anymore. I don't care about anything. And I don't think I'm capable of living with anyone,' he continued slowly. 'I don't think I'm capable of anything but being alone. I haven't got enough feeling left. I'm not sure there's anything left at all.'

'There was a little while ago,' she pointed out with a smile, 'when you didn't want to be alone. You really don't, you know. You only think you do. Trust me, Simon,' she whispered.

'I don't know how,' he said without expression. 'I've never trusted anyone.'

'You trusted me once,' she reminded him.

'I suppose I did,' he agreed absently, 'and look where that got me.' He closed his eyes for an instant and then opened them again, looking uncomfortable. 'I'm sorry. I shouldn't have said that.' He drew a deep breath. 'Victoria, I'm not thinking particularly clearly at the moment, and there's no point trying to settle anything until I am. You've got to give me some time.'

'Are you going to leave me again?' she asked carefully, her eyes never leaving his face.

'No, but you're going to leave me,' he said with an

attempt to be firm. 'You're going back to New York and leave me to get a few things straightened out.'

'So that you can decide that what happened between us just now didn't really mean a thing?'

'I'm not even going to think about what happened between us just now until I see you again.' He smiled self-consciously. 'What I'd like to get straightened out is my leg. It's either hurting like hell, or I'm taking pills so it won't, which makes things blur around the edges.'

'And which has this been?' she asked quietly.

'A little bit of both,' he admitted with a grin. 'And neither one is the way to settle anything. *Will* you give me a little time?' he asked carefully. 'If you want to talk about trust, will you trust me that much, or that far?'

She thought for a few minutes and then drew a deep breath. 'All right. I suppose I've got to start by trusting you. I didn't, last time, and things went very badly.'

'Do you mean that you're not going to argue?' He sounded vaguely surprised.

'I'm going to try to do things differently.' She hesitated for a moment. 'Last time, I let you down. I failed you badly. I promise not to do that again.'

'I believe you. I'll trust you, too.' A small smile played at the corners of his mouth. 'That's something new and different, isn't it? It must be a good sign. Perhaps we've got a future after all.' He reached out and pulled her against him. 'You might kiss me just once more,' he suggested mildly, 'before you so obligingly do as I ask, and leave.'

'And I'd better give you back your passport and your wallet,' she said, suddenly remembering that she still had them. 'I kept them in my pocket, so you wouldn't be able to leave when I was sleeping or downstairs having lunch,' she explained self-consciously as she saw his puzzled look.

'And *you're* the one who brought up this whole business of trust!' He favoured her with a lazy smile. 'You are a devious little thing, aren't you? I didn't stand a chance. Thank God for that,' he added almost absently, just before he kissed her with satisfying thoroughness.

CHAPTER NINE

FOR Victoria, New York was an unpleasant reality, forced upon her far too soon. She had left Simon only with the greatest of reluctance and had endured the flight from Paris in something of a daze. When she left the plane, she found she wasn't prepared for the crowds and confusion and noise of the city. She was still trying to savour the time she'd spent with Simon, the new closeness they had shared. She didn't want the spell to be broken; she wanted to keep her happiness and new-found confidence intact. But the spell was broken with a vengeance when she went to see Tim the morning after her arrival.

She knew precisely what she had to do, so she began without preliminaries as soon as she'd closed the office door behind her.

'There isn't any story.' She met Tim's gaze without flinching, hoping that she could successfully convince him. It was absolutely vital that she not betray Simon. Everything depended on that. 'I had it all wrong.'

'Of course you did,' he agreed dryly, his expression watchful. 'Simon Durant isn't Peter Soule, and never was. The fact that the two of them were so often in the same place at the same time is strictly a coincidence.'

'That's right,' she said evenly. 'I spent a long time talking with him—with Simon, that is—and he explained it all. There isn't any question about it.'

'I should have known,' Tim told her with a sour look.

'Should have known what?'

'How this was going to turn out. When someone is as angry as you were—particularly someone like you, who usually doesn't let anything ruffle her calm—then it's obvious that the person still cares a great deal.'

'That has nothing to do with it,' she said carefully.

'Of course it has! It's written all over your face,' he said sourly. 'That bastard has found a way of getting to you, hasn't he?'

'Don't call him a bastard!' she flared.

'After what he did to you five years ago, and the game I'll bet he's playing now, I'd say that's exactly what he is.'

'Well, he's not,' she contradicted, 'and he's not playing any game.'

'Of course he is. He's obviously found a perfect way to keep you from breaking the story. What did he do? Seduce you again?'

'I think we'd better not discuss this any longer,' she told Tim, her voice cold. 'You don't know what you're talking about.'

'I know that you've got a good story, and that the man has found a way to keep you from breaking it. That means he's very clever, and you're being a fool.'

'I think I'd better leave now,' she said abruptly, getting to her feet.

'Vicky, just give this a little thought,' Tim urged. 'Do you think he'll marry you, if you don't break the story? If you do, then you're even more naive than I thought. And if he does marry you, then all I can say is that it's not a very good basis for a marriage. The worst of it is that it won't do any good. This story *will* come out sometime, you know. It's too good not to. And if he's only married you to protect his privacy, there won't be anything left—no reason for him to keep on being married to you.'

'You've got it all wrong,' she said steadily.

'I think you're the one who's got it all wrong.' He sighed. 'But maybe, if he doesn't make his move immediately, you'll have enough time to think things through and come to your senses.' He watched as she started towards the door. 'Should I ask when you're coming back to work?'

'I'm not coming back to work,' she said quickly, burning her bridges behind her without regret. 'I'm through with *Global News.*'

'You've got to give a month's notice,' Tim reminded her, his voice angry. 'You can't quit yet.'

'Then sue me!' she snapped. 'For breach of contract, or anything else you like.'

'I'll wait a bit on that, I think.' Suddenly, he seemed to soften a little. 'I'll wait to see if you'll come to your senses. If he leaves you alone long enough, you just might. Vicky,' he appealed, 'it's just that I don't want to see you hurt again.'

'I'm not going to be hurt again,' she told him, softening a little herself. 'Honestly, Tim, I know what I'm doing.'

'I hope so,' he said heavily, staring after her as she opened the door and slipped out of his office.

Explaining things to Tim hadn't gone quite as Victoria had expected. It was obvious that he hadn't believed her story, and she bitterly resented his suggestion that Simon was only using her. Still, he'd accepted her decision, and he hadn't threatened to give her information to someone else to use. All in all, she considered that the encounter had gone reasonably well.

When she had finished cleaning out her desk and had left the office for the last time, she was feeling remarkably pleased with her life. The memory of her time with Simon was still fresh, and she had no doubts about him or the decisions she had made. She wasn't worried about Simon's final misgivings about himself. He was wrong if he felt he had no feelings left, that he was only capable of being alone. The two of them had conclusively proved that there was plenty of feeling left, and it was obvious that he didn't want to be alone any longer.

All of that was satisfyingly clear on the day she talked to Tim, and it remained satisfyingly clear for several more days. But the time continued to pass; she heard nothing from Simon and the doubts began to creep into her mind. She fought against them as well as she could. It was a matter of trust, she reminded herself. They had agreed to trust each other and it was vital that she trust him now. She mustn't allow her judgment to be coloured or her feelings to be twisted by irrational doubt. This time she *would* do things differently.

Still, it was hard, and harder still because there was nothing else to occupy her time. Since the summer she'd met Simon, she had worked steadily, but now her time was completely her own. She almost wished she hadn't been so quick to give up her job. She could have gone back and picked up routine assignments, given herself a way to fill the days. But the thought of retaining any ties to *Global News* made her feel vaguely uneasy, as though even the fact of being a reporter was some kind of disloyalty to Simon.

So she waited, trying to maintain her composure and refusing to dwell on what Tim had said about coming to her senses. She *had* come to her senses in a hotel room in Paris, and so had Simon. He might now be having trouble believing that, but he would believe in time.

The question was, of course, how much time it would take. She'd been waiting now for almost two months, and the doubts were becoming increasingly difficult to handle. While she tried to believe, there was always a nagging fear that Simon had decided to actually do to her what she had thought he'd done four years ago.

There would be a certain poetic justice to that, she decided gloomily as she went out late one afternoon for a long and aimless walk. She was spending a lot of time on long and aimless walks, now that the second month of waiting was drawing to a close. Walking filled some of the empty hours and frequently left her tired enough to sleep at night.

But on this day even the weather increased her sense of depression. The crisp, clean air of autumn had now been replaced by the first damp and penetrating cold of early winter. The sky was a leaden grey and the streets bleak and cheerless. She was chilled to the bone by the time she returned to her apartment. But not at all tired, she realised unhappily. She merely felt even more depressed than before, thinking of yet another empty evening stretching ahead. As she unlocked the door and reached for the light switch, the world seemed bleak indeed. Then the telephone rang, the sound of it so unexpected that she jumped.

The telephone never rang these days, and she stared foolishly at it as it rang again. Her only friends had been those at work, and the friendships had been so superficial that they had ended abruptly when she had quit her job. No one could be calling her, she told herself dully, unless—suddenly mobilised, she slammed the door shut, ignoring the light as she raced to the telephone. She answered breathlessly on the fourth ring.

'Where did I get you from?' Simon asked cheerfully, not bothering to identify himself. 'You sound as though you've been running.'

'I only just got in,' she answered automatically and then realised that wasn't important. 'Where *are* you?' she demanded.

'Still in Paris, but I'll be back in a day or two—three at the most.'

'Are you sure?' she asked, her voice wavering slightly as she clutched the receiver.

'Of course I'm sure,' he answered mildly. 'Weren't you?' He hesitated for a moment, listening carefully to her silence. 'Having a little trouble with trust, are you?' he asked, sounding amused. 'It ought to be the other way around, you know. You're the one who brought it up in the first place, that other day in the hotel.'

'That other day in the hotel was two months ago.'

'Was it really?' he asked, sounding genuinely surprised. 'I wouldn't have thought it was so long ago. I'm tempted to say, "How time flies, when you're having fun", but that wouldn't be strictly accurate. What's the matter, Victoria? Have you been doubting me—or missing me? Or perhaps a bit of both?' he offered as an acceptable compromise.

'Well, missing you and being afraid you'd decide this wouldn't work,' she answered honestly. 'I don't think that's really doubting you—it's just being afraid.'

'If it's any consolation, you're not the only one to feel that way. I've been through my share of it, too. The first however many weeks it's been were relatively straightforward. I was in the American Hospital here, and the doctors were amusing themselves at my expense—digging bits of metal out of my leg. Then they had even more fun,' he continued dispassionately, 'when they broke it all over again and set it properly. Being quite so thoroughly worked over does have the advantage of leaving very little room for black thoughts.'

'Was it terribly bad?' she asked quickly, experiencing a pang of conscience as she realised just what he'd had to endure during the past two months.

'I don't know,' he answered impatiently. 'I don't bother to remember things like that. As bad as it may have been, it wasn't nearly as bad as the black thoughts that descended on me five days ago, when I finally got out of the place.

'I holed up, you see, to try to work this business through. I'm very good at holing up and thinking black thoughts,' he explained self-consciously. 'That's what I do best, when I'm not killing time and fighting other people's wars. The trouble was that I didn't seem able to pull it off this time,' he finished abruptly.

'Pull what off?' she asked, not able to tell if he were giving her good news or bad.

'The black thoughts,' he explained carefully. 'Reason says that I ought to believe everything I've told you about why this is too difficult to attempt. I'm still not sure that I'm capable of living with anyone, and it's not fair to expect you to put up with me while I give it a try. But I want to, Victoria,' he said softly, hesitating for a moment. 'And as far as not having any feeling left goes, I seem to have been wrong about that. If anything, I've had too much. I've tried my best to be logical about all this, but I haven't succeeded.'

'I'm not sure it's possible to be logical about love.'

'You might have told me that,' he said almost irritably. 'I've spent four days being torn apart because I was trying to be so incredibly logical, and it wasn't working worth a damn.'

'Wasn't it?' she asked happily.

'You know perfectly well it wasn't, and you needn't sound so pleased.' He paused for an instant and then continued with a certain degree of difficulty. 'I've been so empty for so long, Victoria. I don't want to be alone any longer.'

'I'm glad of that,' she said simply, leaning against her table, feeling limp with relief. 'I don't want to be either.'

'Does that mean you'll have me?'

'Of course I'll have you,' she answered almost

impatiently. 'I don't know why you even bother to ask. You didn't, the last time.'

'Yes, and look where that got us,' he pointed out with ironic amusement. 'Perhaps I ought to say, "Vicky, will you marry me?" but I can't. I absolutely draw the line at that. It's not the marry part of it that bothers me,' he continued, sounding positively light-hearted now. 'It's the Vicky. You're simply not the sort of girl to be a Vicky.'

'I'm hardly a girl,' Victoria felt bound to point out. 'I'm twenty-seven, nearly twenty-eight. I haven't been a girl for years.'

'Well, you always will be, as far as I'm concerned,' he told her firmly. 'Except, of course, when I'm thinking of you as that grand old lady I once assumed you were. That's one of the few incorrect assumptions I've ever made—that and thinking you were a spinster. We'll prove that one wrong as soon as it's legally possible, once I'm back in New York,' he finished with considerable satisfaction.

'And that won't be for two or three days?' she asked with sudden longing. Hearing his voice again made her impatient to have all of him.

'No more than that,' he assured her. 'The doctors want to admire their handiwork a few more times, but I'll come as soon as I can. And one more thing,' he added, as though it were nothing more than a casual afterthought, 'you were right, all along.'

'Right about what?'

'Peter Soule,' he answered impatiently. 'I suppose you could say that's who I am—some of the time, at least.'

'Why are you telling me now?' she asked softly.

'I'm not sure,' he said, sounding almost confused. 'Perhaps because it's the one last loose end, and I thought I ought to dispose of it now. And it wasn't fair,' he continued awkwardly, 'to keep on withholding that one part of myself from you—particularly when you'd known it for so long.'

'I've really only known it since sometime this summer.'

'No. You've known it for years,' he said seriously. 'You knew it within twenty-four hours of when we met. You said there were things you knew about me, without being told. You said they were waiting somewhere in your mind, and I knew you were talking about Peter Soule—that you'd read the book. I ought to have told you then,' he continued uncomfortably, 'but I didn't trust you enough. I was afraid you wouldn't want anything more to do with me, once you knew about that other part of me—the part that was self-indulgent and bragged about my exploits.'

'You should have told me,' she said carefully. 'I wish you had.' She hesitated for a moment and then made a confession of her own. 'If you had, you'd have found out that I'd been loving you since I was twenty.'

'You didn't know me when you were twenty,' he objected, sounding amused.

'But I'd known Peter Soule that long,' she explained, 'and I fell in love with him the first time I read *Under Starlight*. I know it sounds dreadfully adolescent, but he knew about loneliness, too. But his was worse than mine, and I wanted somehow to take his away.'

'And so you have,' Simon agreed unsteadily, and there was a long silence at his end of the line. 'I don't know what I'd do without you, Victoria,' he finally said with an almost frightening intensity. 'I'll be with you as soon as I can.'

He came two days later, although he came so late that she had already given up and gone to bed, assuming that she'd have to wait another day. His knock on the door awoke her from a restless sleep and she switched on the lamp, instantly alert as she ran barefoot across the room to open the door.

He was a tall, dark presence in the narrow corridor, his expression hidden by shadows. She hesitated for a moment, waiting for him to draw her into his arms. But he didn't do that; he merely moved slowly past her into the room.

'I'm surprised you weren't at the airport,' he said carefully, his voice expressionless and sounding very tired. 'I expected to see you there,' he added with a strange inflection.

'But you didn't say what flight you were taking,' she explained from the doorway, eyeing him doubtfully. He had his back to her so she couldn't see his face, but she sensed that there was something not quite right about him. Somehow, the set of his shoulders and the way he was standing suggested both great fatigue and a certain element of nervous energy. 'You weren't even sure if you'd be coming today or tomorrow,' she finished uneasily, wishing he'd turn and look at her.

'Still, you managed to find out, didn't you?' he asked, and the sudden trace of bitterness in his voice confused her.

'I'm not sure what you're talking about,' she said foolishly, because she had absolutely no idea what he meant. 'Is something wrong?'

'You know perfectly well what's wrong. There's no point in trying to play the innocent with me. Although it is interesting that you'd try that particular approach,' he continued, more to himself than to her. 'That's the only reason why I came, in fact—to see how you would attempt to handle this. I rather thought you'd brazen it out, be the cool and self-possessed career girl again, and not give a damn. But perhaps it better suits your image of yourself to play at innocence.' He hesitated for a moment and then turned to stare at her with unseeing eyes. 'Unless, of course, you actually thought you could get away with it,' he added absently.

'I don't know what you're talking about,' Victoria told him, frightened now that she could see his face. It was rigidly set, the planes and angles more pronounced than ever, with an expression of active distaste which reached his eyes. 'You'll have to explain it to me,' she tried again, when he remained silent.

'We both know better than that,' he said savagely. 'For God's sake, stop pretending! It won't do any good at all.' He hunted through his pockets in the old, familiar way, until he found his cigarettes and lighter. Then, with hands which weren't quite steady, he lit one and seemed to regain his composure. 'They were there, of course. You'll be pleased to know that they didn't miss me.'

'*Who* were there?' she asked, her voice trembling in the face of his barely controlled anger.

'*Global News*,' he answered with careful distaste. 'Two reporters and a photographer. That's why I expected you to be there, but perhaps there wasn't any need. You've obviously already filed your story for tomorrow's papers. All they were after was my reaction and a few pictures of Peter Soule. You really didn't need to be there, did you?'

'Do you mean that someone at Global knows you're Peter Soule?' she demanded incredulously.

'*You* know I'm Peter Soule,' he pointed out with a complete absence of expression. 'You already did, but I was fool enough to actually admit it, the other day on the telephone. That was when I thought I could trust you,' he added, looking around until he found an ashtray on the table between the two gold chairs. He bent—a little unsteadily, she thought—to brush the ash from his cigarette and then straightened up as though the action cost him some effort.

'You really ought to have waited longer,' he continued after a moment, staring absently down at the cigarette in his hand. 'You shouldn't have been so anxious to see the story in print. If you'd been willing to be patient, you'd have had so much more to say. I was trusting you, you see, and it was suddenly a relief to think that I could tell you everything I'd never said before.' She saw the brief expression of pain in his face, and then he shook his head. 'Better not to think about that,' he said carefully, bending again to stub out his cigarette. 'Better not to think at all, but I haven't quite achieved that state.' He searched his pockets again and then lit another cigarette with elaborate care.

'You can't believe that I have anything to do with this,' she whispered, staring at him with frightened eyes.

'Oh Lord, I told you to stop pretending,' he said wearily. 'I don't know what you hope to accomplish by it, unless you've still got some mad idea that you can get away with it. Do you really think you can?'

'I don't think anything,' she answered bitterly. 'I don't see how you can believe I do. It doesn't make any sense!'

'I'll grant you that,' he agreed without expression. 'It doesn't make any sense at all, unless you thought you could somehow make me believe you. Did you actually think I would, when you denied it? Did you think I'd trust you that much? I'd be mad to trust you that much,' he finished absently.

'I think you're mad anyway!' she snapped, suddenly goaded beyond endurance. 'It's mad to think I'd agree to marry you, and then do this to you!'

'Right again,' he agreed sarcastically, and now she could hear the anger beneath his words. 'But you must have thought there was at least a chance that you could manage it. God knows why you wanted to, unless you thought I'd be good for a few bedroom revelations and another story.' He carelessly dropped his cigarette into the ashtray and then crossed the room a little unsteadily to stand in front of her. There was something menacing in the way he towered over her, and she backed nervously away until she was up against the wall, unable to retreat further.

'Did you think that I loved you so much that I'd forgive you anything?' he asked with deceptive calm, staring down at her. 'Did you think you'd made me *need* you so badly that I wouldn't care what you'd done?' He moved a step closer, swaying slightly until he put out his hand to brace himself against the wall. Now Victoria felt thoroughly trapped, his arm just above her shoulder and his long form no more than a foot away from her.

'I don't need anyone that much,' he continued after a pause, looking down at her with active distaste in his eyes. 'I don't even need you, in spite of your best efforts. And your best efforts were very good indeed. You must have thought you'd captured me completely after that time in Paris, when you used all your special tricks on me. "No one could make me feel like this," ' he mocked bitterly, throwing back at her the words she'd said to him that day. ' "I can't imagine doing this with anyone but you." It was a marvellous bit of innocence, but just a shade to practised, I think—now that I've had time to consider it more logically. I ought to have realised it at the time, but you saw to it that I didn't—with all your clever distractions. God knows how many times you've done things like that—and more—or with how many other men,' he finished savagely.

Victoria closed her eyes, so sickened by what she was hearing that she couldn't bear to look at him.

'And now this artfully contrived attempt,' he continued sarcastically, and her eyes flew open as she felt his hands fumbling with the straps of her nightgown. 'It's very clever,' he added absently his fingers brushing lightly against her skin.

'Don't you dare touch me!' She stared defiantly at him as she started to edge away.

'But that's obviously what you want me to do.' He smiled unpleasantly as one hand gripped her shoulder, holding her in place. 'What you intend me to do,' he corrected, making a fine distinction as he removed his other hand. 'You must have thought it all out very carefully. No need to come to the airport, and better if you don't. There's a chance that I won't believe that you're a part of this. And if I come to you, you can appear before me, fresh from your bed and leaving very little to the imagination. Just enough to make it interesting and slightly seductive—to see if I can resist you. You must have thought it all out very carefully,' he said again, nodding slowly. 'Does it disappoint you that I have resisted? Would you like to try something more, to see if you can make me give in to you?'

'I don't even want to *talk* to you,' she told him, her voice shaking with anger.

'Of course you don't want to *talk* to me,' he agreed, his words slurring slightly. 'Now's the time to seduce me, and talking's no good for that. Now's the time to slip your arms around my neck and lean against me, trying to drive me mad again with all your clever tricks.'

'You're drunk,' she snapped, as the realisation hit her.

'Not as drunk as I'm going to be,' he said carefully. 'I intend to become very drunk indeed, after I'm done with you. Not because you've broken my heart, or wounded me to the core, or whatever it is you'd like to think you've done to me. I want you to understand that my feelings for you have nothing to do with it. I haven't got any feelings for you—not any longer.' He hesitated for a moment, as though he'd lost the thread of his thought and was having difficulty finding it again. 'It's only that my judgment was so poor,' he finally resumed. 'I pride myself on my good judgment, and I prefer not to dwell on how poor it was about you. Getting very drunk seems the best way of forgetting that. I started as soon as I'd shaken off your friends from *Global News*,' he explained with an expression of distaste, 'and I intend to continue, as soon as I leave here. It was stupid of me to be so wrong about you,' he added for his own benefit, clearly oblivious of her presence for the moment. 'Out of character, too. I'm usually right about things. Almost always right, in fact.'

Victoria bit her lip, anger quickly replaced by pain as she remembered him saying those same words, the night they met. The memory suddenly caused her to grasp the enormity of what was happening to them, and pain twisted within her like a knife. 'Simon, please! Please let me explain,' she whispered, looking up, her eyes pleading with him to understand.

'Nicely done.' He nodded with an air of detachment. 'Unexpectedly subtle. You haven't thrown yourself at me, or even tried to touch me. You've just looked up at me with mute appeal in your eyes, knowing damn well how attractive you are right now. I expect you chose that nightgown with special care, hoping I'd come. It's a fine combination of innocence and—well, I suppose promise is as good a word as any.' He smiled briefly, with cool dispassion. 'It's a nice touch, but it won't do any good. You could try anything you like right now, and it wouldn't have any effect. I wouldn't feel anything at all.'

'You're *afraid* to feel anything,' she cried, shocking herself with her intensity. 'You'd rather believe the worst of me—even if it doesn't make any sense—then give me a chance to explain. You're afraid to care and you've finally managed to find a way to avoid it completely!'

'I'm not afraid of anything,' he contradicted quickly. 'Certainly not of you. I could make love to you right now—let you try all your clever tricks—and it wouldn't mean a thing. I wouldn't care at all,' he added as his hand left her shoulder and brushed lightly against the hollow at the base of her throat.

'You wouldn't dare!'

'I might,' he said carefully, his hand moving slowly lower, following the curve of the neckline of her nightgown. 'Just to prove how wrong you are,' he added absently as his fingers continued to explore.

She was shocked into immobility as he suddenly pushed aside the straps of her gown and both hands began to caress her breasts with slow deliberation. 'You see?' He leaned towards her, his face only inches away from hers. 'I'm not afraid of you. I'm not afraid of anything,' he added, continuing his empty caresses while she stood rigid beneath his touch. 'It's impossible to make me want you. You can't do it—not after what you've already done to me.' Abruptly, he withdrew his hands. 'You see?' he asked again, sounding satisfied. 'It doesn't mean a thing. Nothing at all. I'll do it once more, I think, so you'll be sure to believe me.'

But Victoria had suddenly had enough—more than enough. As he reached for her again, she raised her hand and swung it as hard as she could. Her open palm struck his face with an audible sound, leaving a livid mark behind.

'Perhaps you're right,' he agreed evenly, as though he

hadn't even felt the blow. 'I needn't try again. I've proved my point, haven't I? You can't do anything to me, Victoria. You've done it all.'

'I haven't done anything,' she snapped, struggling to pull her nightgown back in place as he moved away from her. 'I haven't written any stories about you; I haven't even told anyone about you—except my editor, and that was before I went out to Pakistan to find you. I had to tell him, or he wouldn't have let me go.

'But when I got back, I told him I'd been wrong,' she continued, finding a grand release in explaining herself—even if Simon wouldn't believe her and quite possibly wouldn't even listen to what she was saying. 'I told him you weren't Peter Soule, that I'd been mistaken and there wasn't any story. I don't know anything more than you do about why there were Global people at the airport. I even quit my job,' she added unsteadily. 'They may still sue me for breach of contract.'

'But you aren't going to believe anything I say,' she hurried on, gathering momentum again. 'You don't want to believe me. It's safer for you if you don't. I should have known that you weren't capable of trusting me. But you're not capable of trusting anyone. I could have saved us both this particular exercise in futility, if I'd really believed what you told me in Paris.'

'And what was that?' he asked with deceptive calm, giving her the only indication that he'd heard a word she'd said.

'That you're worse now than you were five years ago. You were right about that! You're twisted and bitter and cruel. You deserve to spend your life killing time and not caring about anyone or anything. You're not fit for anything else!'

'Does it make you feel better to try to blame me?' he asked with supreme indifference, but his face was livid with anger and she could see a pulse beating furiously at his temple. He started to speak again and then obviously thought better of it. Instead, he moved past her to the door of the apartment. He didn't even look in her direction as he fumbled for the knob and then left, slamming the door behind him with a resounding crash.

CHAPTER TEN

HE had done it again! Victoria could hardly believe it as she stared at the door Simon had just slammed shut. Incredibly, he had repeated the pattern. He had allowed himself to come just so close before he'd been forced to retreat. He'd needed an excuse, a reason to withdraw from her, and he'd managed to find one—insane though it might be.

He had behaved no differently than he had five years ago, she thought bitterly. Than she caught herself, remembering that night in the hotel in Peshawar, remembering how she'd learned that he *had* intended to come back to her. And he had done so, as soon as he had been able. But had he really come to stay? she asked herself, turning away from the door and beginning to pace the room. God alone knew how Simon's mind worked; she didn't pretend to know, although she spent the rest of the night trying to untangle the mystery.

With the first light of dawn, obeying some impulse she didn't fully understand, she went out to buy the morning papers. Back in the apartment, she made coffee and then settled at the table to see what the articles had to say. There was a certain morbid fascination in learning what had been printed, and in wondering if Simon were doing the same.

The story was very much as she had expected it to be. All the information she had acquired was there: Simon's illegitimate birth, his years as a foster child, and his attempts to get an education. There was special emphasis on his military record, drawing the same parallels with *Under Starlight* as she had drawn. The article had ended by summarising his time with the Afghan rebels during the past summer's offensive.

But the story itself didn't interest Victoria as much as the question of how it had come to be written, and the answer was very simple. The by-line was Ken's, and that made perfect sense. Even before she'd left for Pakistan, Tim had warned her to keep her notes locked away because Ken was nosing around, trying to find out what she was doing. What she couldn't immediately understand was how Ken had managed to learn so much. She *had* kept her notes locked in her desk, and she hadn't told anyone but Tim about the story.

It was possible, she supposed, that Tim had passed the story on to Ken, after she had resigned. But even if he hadn't, there were still ways in which Ken could have learned what her story was. He could have started with Ginny in the research department, and used his considerable powers of flattery and flirtatiousness. It wouldn't have taken that much to get Ginny to give Ken all the details she'd first found for Victoria.

Once Ken had that information, he'd only have needed to make the connection between the known details of Simon Durant's military record and Peter Soule's *Under Starlight*. In a blinding flash, Victoria realised how simple that would have been. From the time she had started working on the story until the day before she left for Pakistan, Peter Soule's two books had been among the clutter on her desk. Not just among it, she admitted ruefully; they had usually been on top of the clutter, there for anyone to see. It was difficult to imagine that Ken would have missed them; he'd been around her desk often enough to notice what was there.

With a connection established between Simon Durant and Peter Soule, Ken had needed only his investigative skills to confirm his facts and provide additional details. It would have been a relatively simple matter, and easier still when it came to the part dealing with Simon's time in Afghanistan. Rahim knew everything she had learned; he'd translated it all for her. He'd have been a marvellous source for Ken, almost as good as her own notes.

So that was probably how it had happened, she thought dully, staring off into space with unseeing eyes. It was Ken who had brought her world crashing down—had brought both her world and Simon's crashing, she corrected automatically. Yet she was forced to concede that it wasn't as simple as that. Ken had been the catalyst, but not the cause of what had happened. She and Simon had done the damage to each other.

Having acknowledged that fact, Victoria waited to begin to feel something; anger or pain or absolute loathing—whatever it was that she actually did feel about Simon for what he had done to her. But she didn't seem to have any feelings left. She was empty inside, completely without emotion. She knew that wasn't natural, and that emotion would come crashing down around her—probably when she least expected it. Until that happened, she was forced to exist in a kind of limbo, eating and sleeping and trying to get through days that were empty as she felt.

It was three days later and—predictably—when she least expected it, that it all came crashing down around her. Out for a walk, she paused to study the items on display in the window of an antique shop just around the corner from her apartment house. As she was about to turn away, a small silver object among a grouping of miniatures caught her attention. When she realised what the object was, she closed her eyes for a moment, overwhelmed by memories. It was a knight in shining armour—a knight-errant, she told herself with such a sense of longing that she could hardly bear the pain. It reminded her too much of Simon, of the time when he *had* been her knight-errant and she had loved him without any doubts at all.

She turned quickly away, torn by conflicting emotions. Tenderness and passion were so mixed with pain and loathing that they could not be separated. Once she had allowed their love to be destroyed by a misunderstanding. Then, given another chance five years later, it had been his misunderstanding which had destroyed their love a second time. She supposed that evened the score between them, but it provided no consolation.

A part of her hated him for that final night when he had refused to believe in her, had refused to listen to her explanation and had then utterly humiliated her. The rest of her was consumed by the attempt to understand how the two of them had managed—not once, but twice—to destroy their love for one another. They *had* loved each other so very much; that was the most painful thought of all. The first time had been the joy of discovery, of learning how much they cared. The second time had been deeper and stronger, as they found themselves bound together by mutual need and understanding.

As she paused at the front door to her building to hunt through her handbag for her keys, she suddenly found herself remembering the afternoon she and Simon had spent in the graveyard on the hill. It was there, in the sunlight, that she had told him he was her knight-errant. That was the day when she had realised that she loved him, the day when she had first begun to learn what passion was. Passion, she had discovered, was far more than physical sensation. Passion was what you felt when you loved someone beyond reason, more than life itself.

She still did love Simon beyond reason, more than life itself. She still did and always would. The realisation hit her with such force that she dropped her keys in the dim hallway and had to search for them. Loving Simon—in spite of everything—was inevitable, a fact of her life which she had to accept without question.

'Hello, Victoria.' She heard his voice in the darkness as she unlocked and opened the door, accepting that, too, without question. It was part of the dream, part of the memory of that afternoon in the graveyard, before anything had happened to destroy what they meant to each other.

But memories weren't reality, and dreams couldn't last forever, so she reached for the light switch. It was time for the dream to end, time to return to reality. The light came on, blinding her for a few moments after the dim hallway. When she could see again, what she saw was Simon—standing by her work table at the other end of the room. Remarkably, he didn't appear to be a dream; he was far too substantial for that.

For an endless length of time, neither of them said anything. Victoria was hopelessly confused, trying to handle two very different and conflicting emotions. The first, of course, was the fact that she loved him. It seemed wildly improbable that she'd only managed to acknowledge that fact as she was about to come face to face with him. But there was a certain inevitability about that: everything about Simon had always had a certain inevitability about it.

The problem was that seeing him again brought vividly to her mind the last time she'd seen him. The memory of the afternoon in the graveyard had been instantly replaced by the memory of his anger and cruelty only a few nights before, in this same room. And just how do I handle all this? she wondered a little hysterically.

'How did you get in?' she asked, because it was the first thing to occur to her. One of them had to say something—they couldn't stand here saying nothing forever, after all!—and one of them had to break the silence.

'I picked your lock,' he answered abruptly, even a little defiantly. 'I didn't think you'd let me in, so it seemed I had no other choice.'

'I see.'

'Well, I'm not entirely sure that you do, but I couldn't think of anything else to do. You really ought to get a dead bolt lock, you know,' he added in a disconcerting shift. 'That thing you have is no earthly good at all. Has anyone ever broken in on you?'

'Not until now,' she answered dryly, taking off her coat and dropping it on the chair beside the door. 'You're the first.'

'It's a wonder.' He sounded surprised. 'I'm very good at picking locks, but yours didn't require any particular skill. It's child's play, and you're really not safe as things stand now.'

'So it would seem,' she agreed, studying him warily and wondering why he'd come.

'It came as something of an anticlimax, once I got in, to find you gone,' he continued, either missing or choosing to ignore her sarcasm. 'I've been waiting for something like three hours, staring at your walls and wondering if you'd left for good.'

'Sorry to have inconvenienced you.'

This time, the sarcasm did register as he gestured impatiently. 'Oh, for God's sake, Victoria, don't fence with me!'

'I don't see why I can't. You broke into my

apartment; you've got no business being here, so I ought to be able to do anything I please. And I wonder what you would have done, if I'd been here when you broke in,' she continued as the thought struck her. 'I might have screamed, or gone after you with a knife.'

'I would have seen to it that you didn't do either of those two things,' he said with a calm assurance which only served to infuriate her.

'Would you have tried some of your guerrilla tactics on me?' she asked bitterly. 'Is that what you mean?'

'Of course not,' he answered impatiently, and then made an obvious attempt at self-restraint. 'I don't really know what I meant, and I don't know what I'd have done if I'd found you here. God knows that I don't know what to do now that you *are* here.'

'You might begin by telling me why *you're* here,' she suggested, surprised to find that it appeared that she was taking this whole thing more calmly than he.

'Well, that's not going to be easy,' he began uncomfortably. 'Would it be putting it too strongly, if I said that I'd come to beg your forgiveness?'

'It would sound a little too dramatic, I think. Almost too extreme.'

'It seems to me that this situation calls for extreme measures,' he said defensively.

'But not *that* extreme, Simon! I'd rather that you just said what you've come to say, instead of begging my forgiveness. Begging doesn't seem your style.'

'I wasn't aware that I had a style,' he said with a quick, dismissing gesture. 'If I did, I haven't got any left. And I've come to tell you that I was terribly wrong, the other night—terribly wrong and unfair. I ought to have been willing to listen to what you had to say; I ought to have known better than to think what I did about you.' He paused for a moment. 'Victoria, I would do anything to take back the things I said and the way I treated you.'

'Would you?' She could hear the pain in his voice and she believed him, but she wondered if there were any way to do what he wanted to do. Suddenly, she wished there were.

'I should have known you weren't responsible for that story,' he continued, rushing his words a bit. 'You were right—it didn't make any sense. I knew that as soon as I was capable of thinking clearly. The problem was that I couldn't think clearly—not just at first. Not until today, in fact. May I sit down?' he asked in an abrupt switch.

She nodded, watching as he walked stiffly to the couch and cautiously lowered himself on to it.

'You see,' he finally resumed without looking at her, 'I've spent most of my life not wanting to face what I am, or the things I've done. You know that better than anyone, because I've told you more than I've ever told anyone else. That's what made you so extraordinary— that I've told you as much as I have. But not everything,' he said wearily. 'There are things I haven't been able to tell you, a few things I haven't even wanted to remember.

'And when I got back to New York the other evening and realised that the story was going to come out, I didn't want to face the thought of it. It wasn't a case of not wanting other people to learn about me. I wasn't worried about Peter Soule's image, or my own. I do assure you of that.' He smiled self-consciously. 'It was that *I* couldn't bear to see it all—all those fresh revelations, day after day. And there were bound to be at least a few of the people I've worked with, through the years, coming forward to contribute even more. Some of them are sure to talk about the things I've wanted to forget. It seemed like the worst possible kind of nightmare.' He shifted uncomfortably and then, for the first time since he'd sat down, looked across at her. 'Can you understand that?'

'I think so.'

'I wanted to blame someone. I was angry, and possibly even a little frightened. I had to blame someone. In a curious way, I thought I could avoid facing it, if I could concentrate on blaming someone else for doing this to me. You were the only person handy,' he explained with a brief expression of apology. 'At that moment, it seemed to make perfect sense to think that you were responsible. But that's only because I wasn't thinking clearly; I wasn't capable of thinking clearly.' He was silent for a very long time while she waited without moving.

'There's one thing more,' he finally resumed. 'When I realised what I'd done to you, I discovered that was worse than having to face myself. It may have been the first time in my life that I wasn't thinking only of myself—wasn't thinking exclusively of myself.' He hesitated for an instant and then shook his head. 'That's not strictly true, because I've been thinking of myself in relation to you since the moment we met. But the point is that I suddenly discovered that you mattered most of all. Facing myself wasn't a pleasant prospect, but it was infinitely better than having to face life without you. The only problem is that I didn't realise that until it was too late.'

'I'm not entirely sure that it *is* too late,' Victoria said carefully.

'Of course it's too late,' he contradicted impatiently. 'I've succeeded in ruining everything! I doubted you; I was unspeakably cruel, and I drove you away. You couldn't possibly want me now.'

'You might let me make my own decision about that,' she told him resentfully. 'You going on about it being too late and my not possibly wanting you back, but you haven't even bothered to ask me how *I* feel about it all.'

'I haven't got any right to ask you,' he said irritably.

'You haven't got any right to make assumptions about me!' she snapped. 'Your assumptions haven't always been right—especially not about me.'

'Haven't they?' he asked, watching her carefully.

'You ought to know that by now!' She stared defiantly across at him.

'Are you saying that you might want me back? That it might not be too late?'

'Well, I'm not, but that's only because you haven't given me a chance,' she said unsteadily.

'Then I'll give you a chance, if that's what you want,' he told her calmly.

'It is what I want,' she said with as much courage as she could muster, 'but it's not quite as simple as that.'

'Of course it's not as simple as that,' he agreed with a suggestion of a smile. 'Nothing about us has ever been simple. Come here, Victoria,' he suddenly commanded, holding out his hand. 'It might go a little more easily if you weren't standing across the room from me. Come here,' he said again when she didn't move, the expression in his eyes compelling her to do as he said.

'It's going to be awfully complicated,' she began uneasily as she sat down beside him, carefully leaving a little distance between them.

'What's going to be so complicated?' he asked patiently.

'What I've got to say.' She twisted her hands nervously 'You just told me that you doubted me and had been cruel and driven me away. And the problem is that I did the very same thing to you.'

'And when did you do that?' he asked, watching her with an abstracted smile.

'When you finally came back to me, four years ago.' She drew a deep breath. The theory was that confession was good for the soul, she thought absently, but it certainly wasn't an easy thing to do. 'Simon, do you remember that I told you I was going to marry someone else?'

'Vividly,' he agreed dryly. 'But you made it clear to me that you didn't, after all.'

'Well, it wasn't true. I just made it up.'

'Did you?' he asked with considerable interest.

She nodded unhappily. 'I lied to you. I couldn't think of any better way to hurt you, and I wanted to hurt you just then.'

'Is that all?' he asked, sounding as though he considered it to be nothing more than a minor point.

'It's quite a bit,' she protested, wishing he'd take the whole thing a little more seriously. 'You've been agonising madly about doubting me and being cruel, but it's no more than I've already done to you. Although you did do it with considerably more flair,' she added after a moment's thought. 'But that's because you do everything with more flair.'

'Flair is a charitable way of putting it,' he murmured uncomfortably. 'I can think of far less pleasant ways to describe it.'

'But it's really the same,' she insisted. 'I was just as cruel to you as you were with me.'

'No, you weren't,' he contradicted gently, drawing her into his arms. 'It's not the same at all.'

'But it is,' she said with as much conviction as she could muster, finding it difficult to continue to argue the point with his arms around her.

'Will it make you happier if I agree with you?' he asked indulgently.

'It might make me feel a little less guilty,' she whispered.

'Then I will, although I think you ought to bear in

mind that you were very young when you did what you did to me. That's an excuse I don't have.'

'I don't think age has anything to do with it,' she objected, lifting her head to look up at him.

'Stop arguing, Victoria,' he said firmly. 'Give in gracefully.'

'But it shouldn't be this easy, and I'm still not sure——'

He effectively silenced her by kissing her with convincing thoroughness. 'You're not sure of what?' he asked when their kiss had ended, sounding amused.

'That you'll trust *me*, now that you know what I did.'

'Of course I'll trust you,' he said with satisfying conviction, gathering her more comfortably into his arms. 'I'll admit that I didn't always—at least not completely,' he told her with a twisted smile. 'But then, I'd never trusted anyone completely. It wasn't until I knew you weren't responsible for the story that everything fell into place. Trusting you isn't a problem now. I'd trust you with my life. I am right now,' he finished softly.

'Oh,' she whispered faintly, trying to resist the urge to cry.

'And I hope that this time—finally—you will believe me,' he continued gently. 'We've both had our problems with trust. It staggers the imagination to consider just how many times we've made a mess of things because we wouldn't—or couldn't—trust each other.'

'I know,' she agreed unhappily. 'We've wasted years, and we wouldn't have had to, if I'd only had more faith in you five years ago.'

'Yes, but it was asking rather a lot of you—to have faith in me when I couldn't give you any explanation of why I was leaving, just when what we both wanted most was to be together. I couldn't blame you for how you felt, but I was trapped. It was absolutely vital that no one know what I was going to be involved in so I couldn't say anything at all.'

'Can you tell me now?' she asked hesitantly, looking up at him.

'I don't see why not. I realise now that you're not going to go off and tell the world.' He smiled self-consciously. 'Still, it's not something I like to talk about. I don't even particularly like to think about it.'

'Because it was such a bad time for you,' Victoria suggested, remembering the night in Peshawar when it had become obvious to her that he'd been captured and tortured.

'Because the whole thing had been *my* failure, from beginning to end,' he contradicted impatiently, even bitterly. 'I'd allowed some of the men I was working with to be captured. At least, I'd been careless enough to allow them to be captured. I think I was already beginning to lose my nerve, or at least the hard edge of it. Even before I met you, I was realising that I couldn't keep on with that sort of life indefinitely. Then, when I did meet you, I realised that I didn't even *want* it any longer. I wanted the sort of permanence and warmth you offered.' He was silent for a long moment, simply holding her close.

'But I'd promised to try to find those men and get them out,' he finally resumed with an obvious effort. 'That's why I felt I had to leave, that one last time. It wasn't just a case of fighting someone else's war. It was an attempt to undo the damage *I'd* done. It had been my responsibility, and I had to try to make it right.'

'Your commitment,' she supplied softly.

He nodded slowly. 'That, and a feeling that I ought to come to you with the slate wiped clean—with no loose ends and that part of my life completely behind me. Only it didn't work out quite that way, did it?' he finished with a twisted smile.

'Because I was too selfish, and wouldn't understand,' she admitted miserably. 'And then, when you did come back, I lied to you and drove you away again.'

'And I went back to fighting other people's wars,' he agreed with an expression of distaste. 'If I'd thought I was losing the hard edge of my nerve, you gave it back to me—with a vengeance. But I'm not blaming you,' he added hastily. 'It was only that I loved you so much that there seemed to be only one way to handle——' He paused, hunting for the words.

'What I'd done to you,' she supplied helpfully, refusing to spare herself by allowing him to be tactful. 'My betrayal.'

'There ought to be a kinder way to put it,' he said uncomfortably.

'There doesn't need to be a kinder way. We might as well be honest.'

'I suppose so. That's trust again, isn't it?' He smiled down at her a little self-consciously. 'At any rate, the only way to handle having loved you so much was to twist it into a towering sort of anger. Which I did do,' he admitted bleakly, 'and went back to fighting other people's wars with singular determination. Besides, there really wasn't anything else to do,' he finished abruptly.

'You did exactly what I did.' Victoria nodded as she suddenly saw the parallel. 'Only I wasn't fighting other people's wars. I decided to be the best reporter *Global News* had ever had. With the same kind of determination, and the same kind of anger,' she added thoughtfully. 'Tim was right.'

'Who is Tim, and what was he right about?' Simon asked, watching her face.

'He's my boss. At least he was, until I quit. When I

came back from Paris and told him that there wasn't any story—that you weren't Peter Soule—he said he might have known. He said that I'd been so angry about you because I still cared very much. It must be inevitable—don't you think? When there's so much emotion floating around, it has to be something. If it can't be love, it has to turn into anger and bitterness.'

'It's good to know we've been caring about each other all these years,' Simon teased with a wry smile. 'Still, we might have managed to enjoy it more, if we hadn't been such fools. Like this,' he added, just before his lips closed over hers and he kissed her with slow and careful deliberation. 'This is better, isn't it?' he asked absently as his lips moved on to find the hollow at the base of her throat.

She nodded, running her fingers through his hair, pulling him even closer. 'You might have been killed,' she whispered, suddenly frightened as the thought struck her.

'But I wasn't,' he murmured, his lips still against her skin. 'So there's no harm done.'

'Promise me you'll never leave again,' she demanded with such intensity that he lifted his head to study her face. 'It's because I don't want anything to happen to you,' she added quickly, in case he didn't understand. 'It's not that I've gone back to being a clinging vine.'

'I know,' he assured her with a lazy smile. 'And I won't leave you. No more fighting wars; I promise you. I'll do the writing I talked about in Paris,' he continued, gathering her closer and cradling her head against his shoulder. 'And you'll do your own writing—at least I hope you will. You're too good to stop. You should have kept at it. Your stories were wonderful.'

'But I couldn't,' she admitted honestly. 'They seemed hopelessly romantic, and I'd stopped being a romantic.'

'Did you?' he asked, almost as though her words

were a challenge. His lips lightly touched her forehead and then moved slowly down the side of her face. 'I don't think you did.'

'No, I don't think I did,' she agreed distractedly as his lips continued to explore. 'And to think this almost didn't happen,' she whispered dreamily. 'If you hadn't seen Ken's by-line, this never would have happened.'

'What do you mean?' he asked absently, his lips flickering lightly against her skin. 'Who's Ken?'

'Ken Newsome—you know. That's how you found out that I didn't break the story.'

'I didn't *find out* that you didn't break the story,' he corrected, lifting his head to smile down at her. 'I just knew that you didn't do it.'

'But didn't you see Ken's by-line?' she asked, now thoroughly confused. 'Isn't that how you knew?'

'I haven't seen any of the stories,' he explained self-consciously. 'I wasn't particularly interested in reading about myself. I haven't seen a newspaper since I got back.'

'Then how *did* you know?' she demanded, staring up at him in confusion.

'Trust,' he said carefully. 'I decided the time had come to trust you completely. That's all it was,' he finished abruptly.

'Oh,' she breathed and then shocked them both by bursting into tears.

'Good Lord! That's no reason to cry, is it?' he asked, appearing more than a little disconcerted. 'You ought to be pleased that I finally learned my lesson.'

'But I didn't know,' she tried to explain through her tears. 'I didn't realise that you just accepted me on faith!'

'But I had,' he told her with a cheerful grin. 'It's what we both ought to have done from the beginning. The only trouble was that neither of us knew enough about this business of trust. And neither of us had enough courage to give it a try. But I know exactly what we ought to have done, to avoid the incredible mess we've made of the last five years.'

'What?' Victoria asked unsteadily.

'We ought to have paid more attention to Susanna Rawson's tombstone,' he explained, sounding enormously pleased with the thought.

'Susanna Rawson's tombstone,' Victoria repeated, pulling herself slightly out of his embrace and wiping her eyes so she could see him properly. 'What on earth does Susanna Rawson's tombstone have to do with all this?'

'Just about everything, I should think,' he said, smiling down at her. 'Don't you remember? I saw it that first day we spent together, when we were having our picnic. And I've been spending the better part of the last three hours studying the rubbing somebody—you, I assume—made of it.'

'I still don't see what it has to do with us,' Victoria told him with a puzzled frown.

'It says, "The heart of her husband safely trusted in her,"' Simon explained patiently. 'That's from the Bible Proverbs, Chapter thirty-one. Grant you, the chapter doesn't say anything about the wife's heart safely trusting in her husband, but I expect she did trust him. He was probably considerably better husband material than I am,' he added in a dispassionate aside. 'But the point of all this is that I might have saved us both a great deal of unhappiness, if I'd only been able to believe that I could safely trust in you.'

'But I was even worse at trusting than you were,' Victoria pointed out quickly. 'This whole mess started because I wouldn't trust you when you left me all those years ago.'

'When you had every reason not to trust me,' he

said gently, 'because I didn't trust *you* enough to tell you everything about myself. *That* was the real problem.'

'But——'

'Don't argue, Victoria,' he told her firmly, drawing her back into his arms. 'It doesn't matter now.'

'I don't suppose it really does,' she agreed, leaning gratefully against him.

'Except that we've both learned a lesson, I think,' he said with considerable satisfaction. 'Hard learned lessons are the best remembered, and I can't believe that any two people have had a harder time at learning a lesson that we have. We're not likely to forget it. And I've decided what I want carved on your tombstone,' he continued in a disconcerting shift. 'It's going to be exactly what Susanna's husband had carved on hers. You may say whatever you like on mine,' he added generously.

'I expect it will be something very similar,' Victoria told him with a demure smile.

'I don't even know why we're talking about tombstones at this particular moment,' he mused lightly, 'except that what it says on Susanna's does mean a great deal to me. Besides,' he continued cheerfully, 'in some obscure way—and my ways are frequently incredibly obscure—tombstones lead back to wedding vows, and the thought of "as long as ye both shall live". It's grand to think of spending the rest of my life with you,' he finished contentedly.

'You're taking it for granted that I'll marry you,' she teased, slipping her arms around his neck and smiling up at him, 'but you haven't even asked me.'

'Of course I haven't,' he answered calmly, returning her smile with an abstracted one of his own. 'The one time I did, a few nights ago on the telephone, things didn't work out too awfully well. I think I'll go back to my original assumption that two people who love each other enough to get married don't need to ask. They already know it's going to happen.'

'*I* didn't know it was going to happen,' Victoria objected lightly. 'I didn't think we stood a chance.'

'Don't argue, Victoria,' he told her firmly. 'You've spent entirely too much time arguing about this whole thing. Besides,' he added carelessly as he bent his head to hers, 'you *must* have known—for the last few minutes, at least.'

'That's true,' she agreed complacently. 'But we'd better do it quickly, before we go and ruin everything again.'

'*That* isn't going to happen, darling girl,' Simon said with complete conviction, just before he kissed her and they lost themselves in the moment and the magic of their hard-won trust.

Hello!

You've come to the end of this story and we truly hope that you enjoyed it.

If you did (or even if you didn't!), have you ever thought that you might like to try writing a romance yourself?

You may not know it, but Mills & Boon are always looking for good new authors and we read every manuscript sent to us. Although we are proud to say that our standards are high and we can't promise every aspiring author success, unless you try you'll never know whether one of those new authors could be you!

Who knows, from being a reader you might become one of our well-loved authors, giving pleasure to thousands of readers around the world. In fact, many of our authors were originally keen Mills & Boon readers who thought, "I can do that" — and they did! So if you've got the love story of the century bubbling away inside your head, don't be shy: write to us for details today, sending a stamped addressed envelope. We'd really like to hear from you!

The Editors

Please write to:

Editorial Dept
Mills & Boon Ltd
15-16 Brook's Mews
London W1A 1DR

The Puppet Master
PIPPA CLARKE
The Iron Heart
EDWINA SHORE
Pacific Disturbance
VANESSA GRANT
Once More with Feeling
NATALIE SPARK

Four brand new titles, from four brand new authors.
All in one attractive gift pack for just £4.40, published on 9th August.
Fall in love with Mills & Boon's new authors.

Mills & Boon

The Rose of Romance

Anne Mather's 100th Romance marks the sale of 100 million of her novels worldwide.

It's a special occasion. And to mark it, here's a special anniversary edition – Stolen Summer, a gripping love story. Beautifully presented, Stolen Summer costs just £1.25 and is published on 12th July.

Mills & Boon

The Rose of Romance

ROMANCE

Variety is the spice of romance

Each month, Mills & Boon publish new romances. New stories about people falling in love. A world of variety in romance — from the best writers in the romantic world. Choose from these titles in July.

MERRINGANNEE BLUFF Kerry Allyne
IMPETUOUS MARRIAGE Rosemary Carter
FANTASY Emma Darcy
THE TROUBLE WITH BRIDGES Emma Goldrick
WHO'S BEEN SLEEPING IN MY BED? C. Lamb
COME NEXT SUMMER Leigh Michaels
RETURN TO ARKADY Jeneth Murrey
AT THE END OF THE DAY Betty Neels
A PROMISE TO DISHONOUR Jessica Steele
EXECUTIVE LADY Sophie Weston
***CYCLONE SEASON** Victoria Gordon
***SAFELY TO TRUST** Avery Thorne

On sale where you buy paperbacks. If you require further information or have any difficulty obtaining them, write to: Mills & Boon Reader Service, PO Box 236, Thornton Road, Croydon, Surrey CR9 3RU, England.

*These two titles are available *only* from Mills & Boon Reader Service.

Mills & Boon
the rose of romance

ROMANCE

Next month's romances from Mills & Boon

Each month, you can choose from a world of variety in romance with Mills & Boon. These are the new titles to look out for next month.

A FOREVER AFFAIR Rosemary Carter
SONG OF A WREN Emma Darcy
EXORCISM Penny Jordan
SLEEPING DESIRE Charlotte Lamb
LIGHTNING STORM Anne McAllister
LOST ENCHANTMENT Margaret Pargeter
WHERE THE GODS DWELL Celia Scott
FRANGIPANI Anne Weale
SUN LORD'S WOMAN Violet Winspear
LOVE IN THE VALLEY Susan Napier
*****MATCHING PAIR** Jayne Bauling
*****WEDNESDAY'S CHILD** Leigh Michaels

Buy them from your usual paperback stockist, or write to: Mills & Boon Reader Service, P.O. Box 236, Thornton Rd, Croydon, Surrey CR9 3RU, England. Readers in South Africa-write to: Mills & Boon Reader Service of Southern Africa, Private Bag X3010, Randburg, 2125.

*These two titles are available *only* from Mills & Boon Reader Service.

Mills & Boon the rose of romance

A romance of searing passion set amid the barbaric splendour of Richard the Lionheart's Crusade. Intrigue turns to love across the battlefield... a longer historical novel from Mills and Boon, for only £2.25.

Published on 12th of July.

The Rose of Romance